PRAISE FOR

THE WINEMAKER DETECTIVE

Twenty-two books
A hit on television in France

"Unusually adept at description, the authors manage to paint everything.... The journey through its pages is not to be rushed."

—*ForeWord Reviews*

"I love good mysteries. I love good wine. So imagine my joy at finding a great mystery about wine, and winemaking, and the whole culture of that fascinating world. And then I find it's the first of a series. I can see myself enjoying many a bottle of wine while enjoying the adventures of Benjamin Cooker in this terrific new series."

—*William Martin, New York Times bestselling author*

"A fine vintage forged by the pens of two very different varietals. It is best consumed slightly chilled, and never alone. You will be intrigued by its mystery, and surprised by its finish, and it will stay with you for a very long time."

—*Peter May, prize-winning, international bestselling author*

"An excellent mystery series in which you eat, drink and discuss wine as much as you do murders."
—*Bernard Frank, Le Nouvel Observateur*

"Perfect for people who might like a little treachery with their evening glass of Bordeaux, a little history and tradition with their Merlot."
—*AustCrime*

"A wonderful translation... wonderful descriptions of the art, architecture, history and landscape.... The shoes are John Lobb, the cigars are Cuban, and the wine is 'classic.' As is this book."
—*Rantin', Ravin' and Reading*

"Benjamin Cooker uses his composure, erudition and intuition to solve heady crimes that take place in the exclusive—and realistic—world of grand cru wines."
—*Jean-Claude Raspiengeas, La Croix*

"I finished it in one sitting! I learned so much about wine making.... But more than that is was a good little mystery—nothing wasted. The book would be perfect for a book club to have a 'wine' night."
—*Bless Your Hearts Mom*

"This is an excellent translation. You never have the feeling you are reading a translated text. The author obviously knows Bordeaux extremely well, and he knows quite a bit about oenology. The book should be a hit with lovers of Bordeaux wine."

—*Tom Fiorini, The Vine Route*

"Combines a fairly simple mystery with the rich feel of the French winemaking industry. The descriptions of the wine and the food are mouth-watering!"

—*The Butler Did It*

"An enjoyable, quick read with the potential for developing into a really unique series."

—*Rachel Coterill Book Reviews*

"A series that is both delectable for connoisseurs of wine and an initiation for those not in the know."

—*Marine de Tilly, Le Figaro*

Treachery in Bordeaux

A Winemaker Detective Novel

Jean-Pierre Alaux
&
Noël Balen

Translated from French by Anne Trager

LE FRENCH BOOK

First published in France as
Mission à Haut-Brion
by Jean-Pierre Alaux and Noël Balen
World copyright © Librairie Arthème Fayard, 2004

English translation copyright © 2012 Anne Trager

First published in English
by Le French Book, Inc., New York

www.lefrenchbook.com

Copyediting by Amy Richards
Cover designed by Melanie Hooyenga/David Zampa

ISBNs:
Trade paperback: 9781939474025
Hardback: 9781939474261
Kindle: 9780985320638
Epub: 9780985320621

*"A bottle of wine contains more philosophy
than all the books in the world."*
— Louis Pasteur

1

The morning was cool and radiant. A west wind had swept the clouds far inland to the gentle hills beyond the city of Bordeaux. Benjamin Cooker gave two whistles, one short, the other drawn out, and Bacchus appeared from the high grass on the riverbank. He had that impertinent look Irish setters get when you remind them that they are dogs. Benjamin liked this clever and deceptively disciplined attitude. He would never roam his childhood landscapes with an animal that was too docile. The Médoc was still wild, despite its well-ordered garden veneer, and it would always be that way. In the distance, a few low wisps of fog were finishing their lazy dance along the Gironde Estuary. It was nearly eleven and time to go home.

The Grangebelle's graceful shape rose among the poplar trees. The building would have seemed bulky, were it not for the elegant roof, the lightly draped pergola, the delicate sparkling of the greenhouse, and the old varnished vases set out in the vegetation with studied negligence. Elisabeth moved silently among the copper pots in the kitchen. She shivered slightly when he kissed her neck. He poured himself a cup of Grand Yunnan tea with slow and precise movements. She knew he was tired. She was perfectly aware of his nights of poor sleep, the deleted pages, the files he relentlessly ordered and reordered, the doubts he had when he completed a tasting note, his concern for the smallest detail, and the chronic worry that he would deliver his manuscript late and disappoint his publisher. Benjamin had worked in his office until five in the morning, taking refuge in the green opaline halo of his old Empire-style lamp. Then he had slipped under the covers to join her, his body ice-cold and his breathing short.

Who could have imagined that France's most famous winemaker, the established authority who caused both grand cru estate owners and unknown young vintners to tremble, was, in fact, a man tormented by the meaning of his words, the accuracy of his judgments, and an objectivity that he brandished like a religious credo? When it came time to hand over a manuscript, his self-doubts assailed him—the man whom the entire profession thought of as entrenched in certainty and science and masterfully accomplished in the fine art of critiquing wines. Benjamin Cooker knew that everyone, without exception, would be waiting for his book to arrive in the stores. They would be weighing his qualifiers and judging his worst and best choices. It was essential that the publication of his guide never blemish his reputation as a winemaker and a sought-after, even secret, advisor in the art of elaborating wines. He made it a point of honor and proved it with his sometimes scathing criticism of wines he himself had crafted. To him, moral integrity stemmed more often than not from this astonishing faculty of uncompromising self-judgment, even when it was forced and terribly unfair. He sometimes thought it belonged to another century, a faraway time, when self-esteem and a certain sense of honor prevailed over the desire for recognition.

He closed his eyes as he drank his tea. He knew that this moment of rest would not last long and that he should make the most of it, appreciating these slow, spread-out seconds. Elisabeth remained quiet.

"Send him to me as soon as he gets here. I need to have a few words with him before lunch," he said, calmly setting down his cup.

Benjamin Cooker dragged himself back to the half-light of his office. He spent more than an hour examining his tasting notes for a Premières Côtes de Blaye and finished by persuading himself that there was nothing left to add. However, his preamble about the specific characteristics of the soil and the vineyard's history was a little short on information, despite his in-depth knowledge of every acre. There was nothing wrong with what he had written, but nothing really specific either. He would have to draw a more detailed picture, refine the contours, and play with an anecdote or two to clarify the text. He did not even lift his eyes from his notes when the doorbell rang out in the hallway. He was nervously scribbling some poetic lines about the Blaye citadel when Elisabeth knocked at the door. She knocked three more times before he told her to come in.

"Our guest has arrived, Benjamin."

"Welcome, young man!" the winemaker said, pushing his glasses to his forehead.

An athletic and honest-looking young man with short hair honored him with a strong handshake that left Benjamin wondering if his fingers would still work.

So you're Virgile Lanssien," Benjamin said, lowering his reading glasses to the tip of his nose.

He invited the young man to sit down and observed him over the top of his lenses for a minute. His dark, pensive good looks would have been almost overwhelming, were it not for the spark of mischief in his eyes. He was dressed simply in a pair of slightly washed-out jeans, a navy blue polo shirt, and white sneakers. He was smart enough not to feign a laid-back attitude when everything about him was on edge. Benjamin appreciated people who did not posture.

"I have heard a lot about the time you spent at the wine school. Professor Dedieu was unending in his praise for your work, and I have to admit that I was rather impressed by your thesis. I have a copy of it here. The title is a little complicated, *Maceration Enzyme Preparation: Mechanism of Action and Reasonable Use*, but your reasoning was straightforward and clear, particularly the section about blind tasting an enzymatic treatment of cabernet sauvignon must. Well done, very well done! Please do excuse me for not having been part of the jury when you defended your dissertation."

"I won't hide my disappointment, sir."

"In any case, my presence would not have changed the result: You greatly deserved the honors you received. I had an emergency call that day to care for some grapevines in Fronsac, and it couldn't wait. The flowering was tricky and required quite a bit of attention."

"I understand, sir. Did you save them at least?"

"More or less. There were enough grapes for me to offer you a bottle," Benjamin said, smiling.

The young man settled into the armchair and relaxed a little. He knew that these formalities foreshadowed a flow of questions that he would have to answer with candor and precision. Benjamin Cooker was a master no cheating could fool. Virgile had read everything written by this man, whose reputation stretched as far as North America and South Africa. He had also

5

heard everything there was to know about the "flying winemaker"—all the scandal monger-ing and bitter words, along with the passionate commentaries and praise. Everything and its opposite were the usual lot of exceptional people, the ransom paid by those who had succeeded in imposing their singularity.

Virgile Lanssien tried to hide his apprehension and answered the sudden volley of questions that descended on him as distinctly as possible. They covered so many topics—layering, copper sulfate spraying, sulfur dioxide additions, microclimates, grand cru longevity, aging on lees, filtering and fining, gravel or limestone soils, fermentation temperatures, primary aromas, and degrees of alcohol—in such disorder, yet Virgile managed to avoid the traps with a skilled farmer's cunning.

"Well, Virgile—I can call you Virgile, can't I? I think that after these appetizers, we have earned the right to a meal."

Elisabeth, wearing a checkered apron tied at her waist, welcomed them into the kitchen.

"We will eat in the kitchen, if that does not bother you, Mr. Lanssien."

"To the contrary, ma'am. May I help with anything?"

"Why don't you set the table. The plates are in that cupboard. The cutlery is here."

Benjamin was surprised to see his wife accept the young man as if he were already part of the family. But Elisabeth knew her man well enough to guess that the job interview was going well.

The winemaker grabbed three stem glasses and poured the wine he had decanted that morning, before the walk with Bacchus.

"Taste this, Virgile."

Benjamin observed his future assistant while he cut the bread and placed the even slices in a basket. The boy knew how to taste. He used his eyes, his nose, and his palate in a natural way, with the attitude of someone who knew more than he showed.

"Wine can be so good when it's good!"

An amused smile crossed Benjamin's lips. The young man had a talent for finding the truth beneath the surface but also a certain guilelessness. Virgile was a cultivated ingénue with enough freshness and spontaneity to compensate for the long years he had focused entirely on his studies.

"I will not be so cruel as to subject you to a blind tasting," Benjamin said, turning the empty bottle to display the label.

"Haut-Brion 1982!" the young man said with a note of rapture. "To tell you the truth, I've never tasted one of these before."

"Enjoy it then. It's harder and harder to grab this vintage away from the small-time speculators who are complicating our lives."

"I made something simple," Elisabeth interrupted, putting an old cast-iron casserole on the table.

Virgile paused, unfolded his napkin, and gave the pot an apprehensive look. Large chunks of eel floated in a thick greenish sauce filled with so many herbs, it looked like a patch of weeds.

"I know, at first glance it does not look very appetizing, but it is a recipe that deserves overcoming your first impression."

"I think I know what it is."

"Lamprey à la Bordelaise. It's a classic," said Elisabeth.

"With this dish, you should always drink the wine that was used in the cooking," Benjamin said, dishing out generous portions. "And nothing is better with lamprey than a red Graves."

Virgile stuck his fork into a piece of eel, dipped it in the sauce and nibbled at it.

"It is first rate, Mrs. Cooker! Excellent."

"And now, let's try a little of this Haut-Brion with that," Benjamin suggested. "Just a swallow, and then tell me what you think."

Virgile did as he was told, with a pleasure he had some trouble hiding.

"It is beautifully complex, particularly with the tannins that are very present. Rather surprising but not aggressive."

Benjamin remained silent and savored his lamprey.

"It leaves a very smooth sensation in the mouth," Virgile continued. "And yet it has a kind of grainy texture."

"Very perceptive. That is typical of Haut-Brion. It is both strong and silky. And what else?"

"It's fruity, wild fruits, with hints of berries, blackberries, and black currant fruit."

"True enough," Benjamin said. "You can taste cherry pits later on, don't you think?"

"I didn't notice, but now that you mention it."

"Beware of what people say. Some may not find that hint of cherry pits, and they wouldn't be wrong."

The guest took the blow without flinching. Benjamin had no trouble pushing his interrogation further. The Pessac-Léognan grand cru loosened Virgile's tongue, and secrets slipped out in every sentence. He recounted his childhood in Montravel, near Bergerac, where his father was a wine grower who shipped his harvest to the wine cooperative and had no ambitions for his estate.

"You'll take over the business one day, won't you?" Elisabeth asked.

"I don't think so. At least not as long as my father is in charge of the property. My older brother is all they need for now to take care of the vineyards."

"That's too bad. Bergerac wines have come a long way and could certainly benefit from your talent," Benjamin said.

"Perhaps one day. I rarely go back, truth be told. Mostly to see my mother, who accuses me of deserting the nest, and my younger sister, who is the only one I can confide in."

He talked a lot, not so much because he wanted to monopolize the conversation, but rather to satisfy his hosts' unfeigned curiosity. To earn his future boss's trust, he felt it was appropriate to answer the Cooker couple's unspoken questions. The winemaker needed to know what was hidden in this excellent and dedicated student. Never had he experienced a job interview that was so informal and piecemeal. He disclosed himself without ostentation, without mystery, and without immodesty. He talked about swimming in the Dordogne River and playing for the Bergerac rugby club, but only for one season, because he preferred canoeing and kayaking. He mentioned his first medals when he joined the swim team, his years studying winemaking at La Tour Blanche, near Château d'Yquem, before he did his military service, and his studio apartment on Rue Saint-Rémi, from which you could see a little bit of the Garonne.

Between two anecdotes, Benjamin went to get a second carafe of Haut-Brion and allowed himself to share some of his own personal memories. It pleased Elisabeth to see her husband finally relaxed and able to forget the tribulations of his writing for a while. Benjamin recounted the crazy, hare-brained ideas his father, Paul William—an antique dealer in London—had and his mother Eleonore's patience. Her maiden name was Fontenac, and she had spent her entire youth here in Grangebelle, on the banks of the Gironde, before she fell in love with that extravagant Englishman who collected old books in a shop at Notting Hill.

Virgile listened. His handsome brown eyes were wide open, and he looked like a slightly frightened child as he began to fully comprehend that this was the famous Cooker, *the* Cooker, whose books he had devoured and who was now sharing confidences. The oenologist enjoyed telling the young graduate about his chaotic career. He had studied law for a year in England, spent a year at the Paris Fine Arts Academy, worked for a year at the Wagons-Lits in train catering and sleeping-car services, and then bartended for a year at the Caveau de la Huchette in the capital before being hired at a wine shop in the fifth arrondissement in Paris, where he worked for three years while taking wine classes.

"The year I turned thirty, I started my wine consulting business," Benjamin said. "Elisabeth and I ended up moving here after my maternal grandfather, Eugène Fontenac, passed away. Since that day, I haven't been able to imagine living anywhere other than Bordeaux."

"That's an unusual career path," Virgile said.

"Yes, it is atypical. I had been around wine since I was a kid, when I visited my grandfather in Grangebelle during summer vacations, but I needed a little time for all that to distill. I had a lot of doubts during my Paris years, and I spent a lot of time searching. I have followed a rather round-about path, but I do not regret any of the detours."

"It's intriguing, like the path a drop of Armagnac takes before it comes out of the alembic."

"That's a fine image," Elisabeth said. "But sometimes it is better not to know all of the mysteries lying in the dark."

"This is one area in which my wife and I differ. I believe you should always seek to uncover secrets."

"I don't really have an opinion on the subject," Virgile said, studying the bottom of his empty glass.

Benjamin Cooker stood up and folded his napkin.

"My dear Virgile, from now on, consider yourself my assistant. We'll discuss the conditions later. I hope that this wine cleared your mind, because I believe you will need all of your faculties. We have a particularly delicate mission awaiting us."

"And when will I be starting?"

The winemaker took a last sip of Haut-Brion and set his glass down slowly. He slipped a hand into his jacket pocket, looked Virgile in the eye, and handed him a set of keys.

"Right now."

2

A few expertly negotiated bends in the road were all it took to assure Benjamin Cooker that he had made the right choice. His new assistant handled the old Mercedes 280 SL convertible with tact. He hadn't needed much time to adjust to it. Virgile had no doubt that handing him the wheel was less a sign of trust than a test. He felt his employer eyeing his slightest moves with a distant vigilance barely masked by the drowsiness that was beginning to slow him down. As they drove through Bordeaux, Benjamin did not regret having let Virgile drive. He was beginning to feel the night of insomnia, and he let the comforting purr of the six cylinders soothe him. The accelerations were smooth, the braking soft, the turns balanced. The boy had to have some hidden fault!

As they approached the limits of Médoc, traffic slowed little by little, until it stopped entirely. The city of Bordeaux was mired in construction. The disfiguring yellow-orange signs looked like they belonged in a cheap carnival. Cranes with empty hooks stood silent, while aggressive insect-like bulldozers lumbered all around them. The tramway—silent, shiny, and bright—would soon rise from this tangled mess. But for now, motorists could do nothing but wait. Some irritated drivers honked without any illusions of being able to move along, while others just put up with it silently.

"We're trapped," Benjamin grumbled. "Take the first street to the right, and let's head to Pessac."

"Are you sure?" asked Virgile.

"Go on. I know a shortcut."

The driver put on his blinker and turned onto a lane lined with gray shops whose scaly facades could have used a serious facelift. The city was being transformed, but it would take much work to restore the gleam of years past. Stonework blackened by pollution would have to be cleaned, and long-neglected facades would need to be uncovered for Bordeaux to find its glory again. Only then could the city open up to the Port of the Moon once more, having shed its rags and come into its own.

Benjamin dictated directions. "Take the second street to the right, then the first left, followed by another left. Straight ahead to the sign. Watch out for the speed bump. To the right. Now, a little farther along, after the blue signs, keep right." Bordeaux's suburbs filed past in a confusion of cubical houses dropped there during the happy-go-lucky nineteen fifties, ugly sheet-metal warehouses and deserted workshops, faux rustic houses with small well-kept yards and mocking gnomes, storefronts, and nineteenth-century working-class homes with stylized figures, sculpted friezes, and zinc festoons.

"We're not far from the wine school," Virgile said, surprised.

"Indeed, it's nearby. At the next light, take the small road that heads downhill. We're almost there."

Benjamin asked his assistant to stop the convertible in the parking lot at the entrance of a large estate that was drowned in greenery and surrounded by a stone wall; shards of broken bottles lined the top to dissuade dishonest visitors. Virgile, who had not asked any questions during the trip, could not contain his curiosity any longer.

"Is this already Pessac?" he asked. "I'm a little lost."

"Yes and no. We're at the Château Les Moniales Haut-Brion. The estate is situated where Pessac, Mérignac, and Bordeaux meet. It is the only vineyard still found within greater Bordeaux."

"Is that so? I thought that there weren't any more on the registry."

"You are quite mistaken! This is one of the intriguing facts about the Moniales Haut-Brion."

"So, it's the last vineyard planted *in* Bordeaux itself?"

"Or the first, depending on how you see things, Virgile," said Benjamin. "Most important, it is owned by one of my best friends."

Before going through the heavy wooden gate that opened to the grounds, the winemaker glanced around, and it seemed that the landscape had changed once again since his last visit some eight months earlier. The estate was locked in by suburban housing developments dating from the happy time before the first oil crisis tarnished illusions. A little farther north, blocks of white subsidized housing rose in stripes against the blue sky, insulting the eye.

Now, right in front of the main Moniales entrance, there were new two-story buildings that already looked like they would age poorly. The architects who designed this tidy, soulless complex clearly lacked taste and culture but had shown a very advanced knack for economy. It was easy to detect the second-rate developer's stinginess in the hastily built structures. No consideration had been given to the families that would take out twenty-year mortgages on homes in this suburb, where the tiniest concrete block was accounted for, the piles of sand measured to the last grain, the woodwork negotiated at the lowest cost, and the gates put up without any grace.

Benjamin entered the estate and immediately headed toward the cellars, which were at the other end of the grounds. He felt at home. Virgile followed three steps behind, not daring to walk beside him, still wondering what they were doing here.

A man of stature was walking in their direction. Benjamin waved at him and turned to his assistant. "Denis Massepain, the estate owner."

Massepain's steps were heavy. But his bearing was that of a natural gentleman farmer devoid of all affectation. He wore a white herringbone shirt, putty-colored pleated dress corduroys, a tweed jacket, and English shoes. Benjamin and he could have had the same tailor. Both had the elegant bearing that comes from being born into well-to-do families. Nearing the age of fifty, neither had concerns about fleeting trends. Denis was an old friend, one Benjamin did not need to see often to feel as close to as he had the day they had met. From time to time, they crossed paths, getting together with their families for an evening in Grangebelle, meeting for a long lunch, just the two of them, at Le Noailles in town, or seeing each other briefly during a tasting among experts. Luckily, Elisabeth got along well with Thérèse Massepain, the daughter of wine merchants from the Chartrons neighborhood. She too had high-born elegance and reserve.

They were a charming couple. Their children were educated, and their company was always pleasant. Benjamin was pleased that Denis had married so well. It was as if Thérèse's smile and the pearl necklace she always wore brightened him up. He had studied to be an embryologist and had worked for a long time for a large pharmaceutical company in Castres before he took over operations at Moniales Haut-Brion, which belonged to his in-laws. Denis had finally put away his test tubes and potions to dedicate himself to presses and oak barrels. He worked hard, was blessed with a pragmatic approach, and was extremely rigorous in his winemaking. It took him only a few years to make this wine one of the most prestigious in the appellation.

"Benjamin, it's a disaster!"

"Hello, Denis."

"A total disaster!"

Benjamin knew his friend had an abrupt nature, but to not even greet him?

"Smell that!"

The winemaker carefully sniffed at the vial that Denis held out. He paused.

"I'm going to be very honest with you," the winemaker said right out, wrinkling his nose. "This is the worst kind of smell. It's a real mess, and you never know how the wine will turn out."

"Are you thinking the same thing I am?"

"I'm afraid so," Benjamin grumbled, moving his nose away from the flask.

"*Brettanomyces*?" the estate owner stammered with a worried look that seemed to refuse the answer that he already knew was obvious.

"I'm not going to hide anything from you. And it seems to be very advanced already."

"I don't understand. It happened all at once. I went to Germany for a week, and when I came back, I found four barrels like this."

"Denis, you are not the first to be the victim of this kind of thing. But it is rather rare to find a Brett infection in a winery of your standing."

"That's why I called you so early this morning."

Absorbed as he was, Denis Massepain had been oblivious to Virgile's presence. Now he took notice and glared at him with suspicion.

"Virgile Lanssien, my new assistant," Benjamin said to reassure his friend before going into the cellars.

"Pleased to meet you," Denis muttered.

"The pleasure is all mine, sir," the young man said, forcing his voice a little.

They followed the winemaker, who had already started ferreting among the barrels. The cellars, which had recently been renovated and enlarged, were kept remarkably clean. There were small one thousand- to two thousand-gallon tanks used to ferment grapes from each parcel separately. The wine was then aged in oak barrels for about eighteen months before being bottled. The small Moniales estate had long lingered in the shadows of the prestigious Château Haut-Brion and its neighbor, Mission Haut-Brion, yet it could now easily rival the best vineyards in the Pessac-Léognan appellation.

Denis Massepain was aware of the challenges and duties the Haut-Brion name imposed on him, so he had called on the advice of experts, notably André Cazebon, an eminent researcher and dean of the Bordeaux Wine School. Benjamin had great esteem for this specialist in monitoring phenolic maturity. He had perfected a technique that made it possible to precisely determine grape maturity so that the fruit could be harvested at the optimal time. With this, the winemaking process could be adapted for each tank, and unique results could be obtained from each parcel.

"Did you tell your wizard?" asked Benjamin.

"I wouldn't have bothered you if he had been around. I think he is in Lyon for a conference."

"We'll need his opinion. I'd like to talk it over with him."

"I haven't been able to reach him."

"We'll take samples from all the barrels, and we also need…"

"It's done already," Denis interrupted. "I prepared a sample from each barrel."

"In that case, I'll take everything to my lab and ask them to fast-track the tests."

"I would like this to stay between us," the estate owner said with a sigh.

"Who do you think we are? It seems to me that Cooker & Co. has a reputation for being more than discreet!"

"I'm sorry, Benjamin. That's not what I meant."

"Virgile and I will be the only ones who know. We won't use any labels or names, so nothing will leak out. Don't worry."

Benjamin gave Virgile a nod, and the assistant effortlessly hoisted the crate full of numbered flasks from the small stainless steel table. Virgile followed his employer, who continued to talk with the master of the Moniales, as they left the cellars and walked up the central drive on the grounds.

"Virgile will come back tomorrow to take further samples from the barrels that are still healthy. In the meantime, you have to isolate the four contaminated barrels," Benjamin advised. "That is a basic measure, and it needs to be done quickly. Better safe than sorry! You don't have to walk us to the gate. I know the way."

The two friends shook hands without saying anything further. His arms around the wooden crate, Virgile took leave of the estate owner with a nod and a smile that tried to be encouraging.

"This estate is really magnificent," the young man said, looking around at the large trees dotting the grounds that had been designed by Michel Bonfin, the landscaper who did the Chartreuse Cemetery in Bordeaux.

Virgile did not hide his admiration. He stopped for a moment to contemplate the Moniales Haut-Brion manor house, built on a hill in front of the cellars. It was surrounded by rows of grapevines and dominated the landscape without arrogance. The château was not huge, but the balance of its slate roof, the curve of its front steps, and the proportions of its facade, with wings that had white Doric columns on both sides, gave the building elegance. A creek called the Peugue flowed at the foot of the knoll, ending among the loose moss-covered cobblestones of a fountain. A small Baroque chapel, built in the seventeenth century, with a pink marble-encrusted pediment, stood in the shade of a chestnut tree. Flocks of birds chirped in the pale April light, and leaves rustled in the breeze.

"It is hard to imagine such a place in the middle of the city."

"It's a small piece of paradise, my dear Virgile, with a whiff of sulfur in it."

"I get that impression too, sir," the assistant said, arranging the samples carefully in the trunk of the car.

Benjamin drove back. They had to move quickly. Very quickly!

3

Benjamin rubbed his eyes. Once again, the night had been short. He gulped down half a teapot of Grand Yunnan, took a very hot shower, splashed on a healthy dose of Bel Ami aftershave, and dressed quickly, not really choosing his clothes. He had spent the entire night rereading his tasting notes, and he had a sharp pain in his lower back.

Elisabeth was still sleeping when he let Bacchus leap into the convertible. The setter sat in the passenger seat, his nose to the wind, a proud look in his eyes, and his ears perked to the understated accents and streamlined drama of a Gluck opera. Benjamin whistled the first measures of *Iphigenia in Taurus;* he was out of tune, but his heart was in it. This was his favorite opening of all, not because he thought it greater than the major works by Mozart or Verdi, but because it was concise. Benjamin had a predilection for openings, prologues, and introductions, whether they were symphonies, oratorios, or lyrical works. He had recorded many tapes and enjoyed them the same way he enjoyed a bottle of wine: for the pleasure of tasting, without feeling obliged to finish it.

The drive was short between Saint-Julien-Beychevelle, where Grangebelle was nestled, and the pier in the small port town of Lamarque. Benjamin drove the nine miles slowly to savor the crisp morning air and make the most of the always-comic show his quivering dog put on, his impertinent snout up to take in the view. The car was quickly loaded on the Médocain, a modern functional ferry stripped of all poetry. Benjamin felt nostalgia for the old captain, Commander Lemonnier, who skillfully piloted a straight-from-the-past boat called Les Deux Rives, an ancient pot-bellied tub whose curves became graceful when, in the hands of a real sailor, they caressed the sea foam. Lemonnier, a former Cape Horner and a formidable master mariner, had started piloting this fresh-water crossing between inland Médoc and the Blaye citadel when he was well beyond seventy. He was capable of steering his boat through fog and dark nights without using any sophisticated navigational instruments. All he needed was a compass, a chronometer, and a tide schedule to avoid the mud banks and skirt the treacherous islands of Île Verte and Fort Pâté, with its headlands. It took him barely twenty minutes to reach the other bank, and it was a pleasure to watch him in the wheelhouse, examining his little black Moleskine notebook, where

he had noted maneuvering speeds and course du-
rations, giving orders with a authoritative voice,
and landing at the pier without even lifting his
eyes from his chronometer's silver box.

The other side was a foreign land, a place
that you could reach with a cannon ball, if not
with the lob of a slingshot. Like the kids from the
Médoc, young Benjamin had dreamed of bloody
attacks, galleys in distress, pirate raids, toothless
buccaneers, and wild mutinies when he had spent
summers here. And after a stormy night, when
the current carried knotty peat, empty containers,
and puffed-up plastic bags, he could still imagine
combats and skinned corpses, their bellies filled
with saltwater.

As soon as Benjamin landed on the right
bank of the Gironde, he had the same feeling
of adventure that had captivated him when his
grandfather Eugène had taken him to visit Blaye.
He parked the convertible in a downtown lot and
headed toward the citadel. Bacchus barked and
had already gone through the king's gate when
Benjamin started over the bridge leading to the
ramparts.

Their walk continued for two full hours.
Dog and master explored the fortress at great
length: the Minimes Convent, the barracks, the
prison and the powder magazine, the Dauphine
counterscarp, the Liverneuf gate, the central pa-
vilion, and the fortified flanks. Benjamin perched

on the Cônes stronghold, pausing for a long time to watch the estuary's slow-moving muddy water. He stared at a swirling eddy in the distance, then set his gaze on a sailboat before eyeing some lone branches washing against the foot of the cliff. Afterward, he climbed the Eguilette tower and took out his spiral notebook. He unscrewed the top of his fountain pen and jotted down some notes in his precise, swirled writing:

Vauban, a man from Dijon (develop this idea)… the two visits from the King (check the dates)… Fort-Médoc kids… fishing for freshwater river shrimp… plaice fillets, court-bouillon (recipe with fennel)… Roland de Roncevaux (be concise)… do not forget Ferri, layout of Fort Pâté… arms factory, troop housing… the water is yellow, brown even, flowerbeds of the houses on the right… shops without giving any details, clock above the bridge, stone watchtower.

He crossed out "stone" and replaced it with "suspended."

It was nearly noon when he turned back toward the middle of town. Bacchus was thirsty and was beginning to show signs of fatigue. Benjamin walked over to a cast-iron fountain and knelt beside the running water, cupping his hands to catch it for his dog to drink. They had enough time before the next ferry to visit an antique shop downtown. As soon as they passed through the beaded curtain, a lean man greeted them. He had the profile of a wading bird, as though he were an ancient hieratic sculpture carved in dry boxwood and lost among the shop's odds and ends.

"Mr. Cooker, I was just going to call you."

"You say that every time, my good man. One of these days I'm going to end up believing you," teased the winemaker.

"No, I mean it. I just received some marvels that have your name all over them."

"Show me your latest finds, but let me warn you, I did not come to Blaye to hunt for antiques. I do not even have checkbook on me."

"Who even mentioned money?" the shopkeeper asked with a wily look in his eye. "Take a look, just for fun. And of course, if you have a little weakness for it, you can pay me later."

"Who says I have weaknesses?"

The secondhand goods dealer unlocked a storage trunk lined with tarp and took out a brightly colored enameled-metal plaque depicting a wine from Saumur. Benjamin was among his best customers, or at least one of the most loyal, and the dealer knew he collected all manner of objects having to do with vineyards and wine. He had already sold him some fine pieces, notably still lifes full of bunches of grapes brightened with tin pitchers, well-made seventeenth- and eighteenth-century paintings, several mythological engravings of Bacchanalia, and various antique corkscrews from all over, some of them

27

very rare. Among Benjamin's finest acquisitions were two well-preserved posters from 1937, one drawn by a certain A. Galland for the Ministry of Agriculture, which touted French wines for "health, gaiety, and hope." The other one was created by Jean Dupas and glorified the city of "Bordeaux, its port, its monuments, and its wines." It had a naked woman standing between the steeple of Saint-André Cathedral and a column generously endowed with clusters of grapes, from which emerged an ocean liner ringed with steam and an old sailboat. These posters brightened the winemaker's offices at 46 Allée de Tourny in Bordeaux.

"I already have this plaque," the winemaker said, somewhat disappointed. "It is very beautiful and typical of the period between the two wars. It looks a little less rusted than mine, but one is enough."

"Well then, I also have a magnificent tun barrel lock that could interest you."

"Magnificent! A *barre de portette*. This was used to keep the small opening at the bottom of a large cask closed. It is really beautiful!"

Benjamin brushed the bronze plate lightly with his fingers. It was decorated with two stylized fish crossing their fins and rubbing their scales in a wave-like movement. The bolt was attached to a wooden support that had the patina of age, but it worked perfectly.

"Are you going to charge me too high a price for this, as usual?"

"I haven't shown you everything yet," the salesman whispered with a mischievous look.

He slid his tall, emaciated body between two armoires and came back with an average-sized painting he placed in front of Benjamin.

"And what do you say about this?"

Benjamin remained silent, although there was much to say. He had been looking for this type of representation for quite some time. It was clear that the canvas dated to the end of the nineteenth century. A stocky winemaker armed with a glass pipette was standing next to a line of oak barrels. A candle on a stool brightened the cellar. The simple balanced composition, the fluidity, the blended colors, and the steady strokes gave this work a timeless feel while placing it in a clear framework. The man's clothing was the only element that spoke of the period, while the entire scene had the scent of eternity. How many times had Benjamin found himself in exactly the same position, among the casks, pipette in hand, sampling wine in nothing but candlelight?

"Do you even dare put a price on this painting?" the winemaker inquired without looking up.

The antique dealer dared and even quoted an amount high enough not to bear repeating.

"You know I don't like to haggle. I have always found that to be somewhat vulgar, but nonetheless…"

"Neither do I, and there is no discussion," the salesman said with a tact that Benjamin appreciated. "That is why I'll give you the barrel lock if you take the painting."

There would be no more bargaining. Benjamin left carrying both items and promised to send a check within the week.

The crossing home seemed longer than it had on the way over, but as usual, the ferry took only twenty minutes to reach the Médoc embankment. Had he gone by land, the drive to the Aquitaine Bridge would have cost him an hour and a half.

Benjamin was eager to show Elisabeth his purchases. She liked the painting but made a face when she saw the bronze lock. Still, she was glad that he had not come back with yet another grape-harvesting basket, wooden topping-up utensil, or silver tasting cup.

The evening was pleasant. Bacchus recovered from the day's excitement in front of the fireplace, where a fine blaze was crackling. The couple enjoyed a tête-à-tête with a meal that was simple enough to allow them to get to bed early.

When his wife had finally fallen asleep, and he felt her calm breathing, the winemaker got up quietly, put on a robe, and went to his office. He checked the ink cartridge in his fountain pen, placed a blank piece of paper at a slight angle under his left hand and began to write about the Blaye citadel.

"History sometimes has an irony that's worth recalling. The land of Bordeaux owes its salvation to a child of Burgundy. When King Louis XIV ordered Vauban, who was born in 1633 in Saint-Léger-de-Foucheret, to build a fortress, several projects had already been…"

Benjamin sighed. A bad start. Not entirely useless, but a little heavy-handed. The city of Blaye had already made it through several centuries before the man from Burgundy unrolled his plans. Yes, Vauban did leave behind a ninety-four-acre fortress with a 2,640-foot-long wall around it and underground passages to protect two thousand people, but violent confrontations had reddened both estuary and dry land before Vauban had built the rough-and-ready bastions.

He opened the cigar box at the corner of his desk and lit up a sweet San Luis Rey robusto, drawing in a deep puff with great pleasure as he leaned back on the headrest. The vitola immediately delivered spicy flavors of green pepper and cinnamon. The smoke, which was not too ample, rose up, round and light. The tobacco was not strong, but developed an aromatic richness in which he could easily discern honey, caramel, and cacao. Benjamin remained in the same position for over half an hour, his mind elsewhere. Then he returned to his pen.

Blaye is called Bordeaux's first rampart. Much is said about this rocky headland. Many popular legends and a few invented stories surround it. Some say that its name comes from the Latin *belli via* (translation: war road); others affirm that a Gallic warrior named Blavos (Blavius in Latin) founded it; people also talk about Blavia, a Celtic word that landed here on the battle path. In any case, Blaye's history is above all..."

Benjamin started yawning. The muscles in his back were sore, and his eyes were stinging. He set down his pen without capping it, crushed out his half-smoked Havana in the ashtray, turned out his lamp, and joined Elisabeth, who, snuggled in the warmth of the comforter, grumbled when she felt his cold body.

4

After answering a few letters from some persnickety readers, filling out a check for the antique dealer in Blaye, checking with his secretary to make sure that the invoice registry was updated, and planning several meetings for fall with Beaujolais estate owners, Benjamin Cooker left his office on the Allée de Tourny and walked to the laboratory he had set up on the Cours du Chapeau Rouge. Virgile was early and had introduced himself to the staff. By the time his employer came in, the assistant was already deep in discussion with Alexandrine de la Palussière, who was in charge of biological testing.

"I see you did not waste any time getting to know each other," Benjamin commented, catching his breath.

"Hello, Mr. Cooker. You didn't take the elevator?" asked the young woman.

Virgile Lanssien shook Benjamin's hand, taking care to control his grip.

"Don't worry, Alexandrine, I'll survive," the winemaker said, still panting, his hands on his lower back. "It will be my only workout for the entire month."

Alexandrine de la Palussière was a discreetly elegant Bordeaux woman who often wore clam-diggers, showing off her tanned calves. She was around thirty, of average height and delicate, with a small upturned nose, green eyes, and bob-cut auburn hair held back with a clear mother-of-pearl headband. On this day, she was wearing a white blouse with the first two buttons astutely undone and a pair of beige leather flats. She was the last child in a line of fallen aristocrats and was not afraid to depart from the rules of her rank by pursuing advanced studies and working like a common mortal. In times past, her family had owned several acres of vineyards in the Haut Médoc, dominated by an enormous châ-teau. Her grandfather had ended up squandering this inheritance in Biarritz casinos and the posh bedrooms of high-class prostitutes. Unlike some penniless petty nobles who clung to appearances, this young woman bore no resemblance to the "dying race" that could still be found in Bordeaux. She was bright, pragmatic, and unpretentious, satisfied to contribute her scientific knowledge to the world of wine that had for so long enriched and nourished her family.

"Where do things stand, Alexandrine?" the winemaker asked when his breathing had returned to normal.

"I need five to eight days to get a reliable colony count."

"That is way too long!"

"But that is the time needed to correctly isolate the yeast and take a count."

"You've gotten me used to miracles. We need to find a quicker solution, even some sort of emergency response, if possible!"

"I can't make any promises, but we could possibly get quicker results by combining plating with a direct colony hybridization. We'll need to use a specific sporulating Brettanomyces probe coupled with peroxidase. After membrane filtration and culture, in forty-eight hours I should be able to tell you if I can detect the micro-colonies."

"Please, Alexandrine, make things simple!" Benjamin cut in.

The young woman's green almond-shaped eyes showed a trace of irritation.

"Mr. Cooker, you know well enough that it is never simple to make things simple!"

"I'll grant you that," Benjamin said in a softer tone.

"What I can tell you is that there is no doubt about the nature of the contamination."

"There's no mistaking that smell of horse piss," said Virgile.

Alexandrine ignored the comment and continued. "The smell of ethyl phenol becomes clearly perceptible once you reach six hundred micrograms per liter. I believe there's an even greater concentration in the samples you brought."

"Do you need more samples?"

"It would be interesting to follow any changes on a daily basis while we are waiting for the first results."

"Virgile will take care of that."

"With pleasure," the assistant murmured without turning his attention away from Alexandrine.

"If I use a consistent approach, I should be able to get a rather reliable quantification, although I won't be able to discriminate perfectly between the living and dead cells, but it would be a good start. An increase in the concentration of phenols would certainly allow me to determine the threshold of alternation, and we could come up with a response strategy," she said.

She perceived worry underneath the winemaker's imperturbable stiff upper lip. In response, she shrugged and shook her head, telegraphing that she wished she could say more.

"The only decision you can make today is to isolate the contaminated wine."

"Thank you, Alexandrine. I would like you to be the only person working on this case. Handle it personally, and make sure that it stays confidential."

"Of course, Mr. Cooker. You can count on me. I do not know the owner of this estate, but tell him that we will find a solution."

"I will try to reassure him."

"In any case, insist that he do nothing until I have defined the exact pH of the wine, the oxidation, and the colonies. He needs to avoid sorbic acid at all cost. It is totally ineffective in red wines, because it is very unstable in the presence of the high levels of lactic acid bacteria found in reds."

"Call me as soon as you have something new," the winemaker concluded.

Then he quickly made the rounds in the offices to greet the other staff members and introduce Virgile Lanssien. He couldn't help pausing for a moment at the windows that opened onto the port, and then he reviewed the results of urethane-concentration tests that had been done on stone-fruit brandy. He scanned the report without going into the details, which covered the carcinogenic risk linked to urethane and fruit purees.

When it came time to leave the lab, he found Virgile doing his best to engage Alexandrine. He signaled that it was time to leave and walked out to the landing. His assistant was quick to join him.

"I understand your attraction, Virgile," Benjamin said in a low voice. "But you would be wrong to pursue her."

"Is that so?"

"I think that boys have little effect on her."

"Are you saying she's…"

"I think that she is more moved by my secretary."

"I never would have thought it. And I usually have a nose for detecting that kind of woman."

"Virgile, think about getting your nose out of the glass from time to time."

§ § §

The Rue des Faures smelled of lamb. The heavy aroma of spices and grilled meat rose up in thick swirls from the hodgepodge of Arab shops, suitcase stores, and faded bistros. Benjamin pretended he was lost in the small streets weaving through the Saint-Michel neighborhood, lingering a little to take full advantage of the moment and enjoy the few stolen hours away from the upscale atmosphere in the Quinconces quarter.

Virgile had returned to the Moniales Haut-Brion with instructions to carefully monitor the sample-taking process. They would meet around ten in the morning to come up with a battle plan to fight the yeast, whose presence the winemaker was having trouble explaining.

Benjamin was holding the painting he had bought in Blaye against his chest. He had wrapped it carefully in brown paper and was on his way to Pascale Dartigeas's restoration workshop near the Passage Saint-Michel. He pressed the doorbell and was greeted by the recorded croaking of a tree frog, which had replaced the original chimes.

"Come in, Mr. Cooker!"

Pascale Dartigeas appeared in a long white smock, a dainty paintbrush in her hand and a rebellious lock of hair hovering on her forehead. She was a beautiful forty years old. When she smiled, crow's-feet appeared at the corners of her blue-gray eyes, and pretty dimples emerged in her cheeks. She showed the signs of a woman who had experienced a lot of unrestrained, selfless love, along with intense joy and periods of abandonment. She had certainly been disappointed by the thoughtlessness of men.

"Hello, Pascale. You look well today."

"Thank you," she said, brushing the hair off her forehead. "I hope you are not here for your overmantel panel. It won't be ready before the end of the month, if all goes well."

"Don't worry. Take your time. I only came to show you my latest extravagance."

"Extravagant people feel very much at home here."

Benjamin carefully removed the brown paper and showed his painting with a satisfied smile.

"What do you think of that?"

"I have nothing to say, Mr. Cooker. It is more than charming. It is…"

"…just what I love," the winemaker interrupted.

"I have no doubt about that, but mostly, it's surprising. I mean, it's very curious. Have you noticed the man's face?"

"What's in the man's face? Is something wrong with it?" Benjamin grumbled, suddenly worried.

"Nothing serious, but it doesn't look like it was part of the original painting. I think it has been repainted. It's a rough job and not very recent, but it was added by another painter."

"Are you sure?"

The art restorer called out to her intern, who was working in the back room, and asked her to bring a black light.

"Let me introduce Julie, who is doing her apprenticeship."

Benjamin nodded at the young blond with big blue eyes. The cleavage of her small breasts and her long legs molded into a pair of tight jeans would certainly have driven Virgile wild. The apprentice flashed an ambiguous smile that threw the winemaker off a little. Pascale Dartigeas took the Wood's lamp from her and ran it above the canvas. A dark stain appeared. All three of them leaned over the painting as she repeated the operation several times.

"There is no doubt. It has been repainted. I propose that we clean it up and see what's underneath.

Julie can start on that later today. Of course, that is if you will allow her to get a little behind on your overmantel, because she is the one who is working with solvents right now. For the time being, I'm touching up the wings of this Baroque angel you see over there, and I don't have time to do the cleaning myself."

"No problem, Pascale, I trust your judgment. And my overmantel appears to be in good hands."

The apprentice, who was either timid or just reserved, ran her tongue over her teeth. She seemed ready to say something but was second-guessing herself.

"What is it, Julie?" Pascale said.

"Have you talked to Mr. Cooker about the second overmantel?" the intern asked in a soft voice.

"Oh, of course, what was I thinking?" said the art restorer. "I almost forgot to tell you that Julie worked on an overmantel that was identical to yours when she did her internship with my colleagues on the Rue Notre-Dame.

Benjamin appeared irritated by this news. He had been certain that it was unique. He would demand an explanation from his antique dealer in Blaye soon enough, but Julie's steady voice and blue eyes calmed him. There was grape harvesting, with people in the rows of grapevines, a small creek and rather tall, very green trees on the side, along with a manor with ocher-colored walls at the bottom. Yet even though the cracking and snail-shaped scaling were similar, the paintings were not exactly the same. No doubt the same painter had done both overmantels. The aging, impasto, traces of mold, gaps, and colors she had to regenerate all corresponded.

When she finished talking, Benjamin had trouble detaching himself from her blue eyes, which seemed to grow brighter and brighter as her face became more animated.

"Do you know the owner of the overmantel, Mademoiselle?" he asked, visibly excited.

"It belongs to Dr. Bladès, an ear-nose-throat specialist who works in the Saint-Gènes neighborhood. I think his office in on the Cours de l'Argonne."

"I'm curious to see this overmantel. Can you see the little chapel near the manor house?"

"No, and it is just that detail that gives character to yours. Particularly the edge of the facade, which is especially delicate," Julie said.

"It is the Mission Haut-Brion chapel. Monks dedicated it to the Virgin Mary toward the end of the seventeenth century. There is no mistaking it, and I agree with you, it gives the painting character."

"I took a picture of your overmantel before we started working on it, if you are interested," said Pascale Dartigeas. "I'll lend it to you, but you'll have to remember to bring it back for my records. In the meantime, what do we do with this repainted face of your cellar master?"

"I don't know. Do your best, as always!"

"In that case, I have a proposition for you. We could do a portrait of you and replace the man's face with yours. This was what people used to do, and I'm sure that this man has taken on the various identities of each one of the painting's owners."

The winemaker found the idea amusing and promised to come back with a picture for the restorer to use as inspiration. Then he asked if he could consult one of the eight volumes of the *Benezit Dictionary of Artists* to determine who was behind the painting's signature. It was a certain T. Roussy, whom he found quickly on page three ninety-five of volume seven covering artists with names between "Poute" and "Syn," as shown in gold lettering on the spine of the book, which was the color of wine lees. Benjamin removed the cap of his fountain pen, took hold of his spiral notebook, and leaned over the table to jot down the information.

"Toussaint Roussy, born in Sète (Hérault) in 1847 (French School). Studied at the School of Fine Arts. Curator at the museum in Sète. His career began at the 1877 Salon. The Sète museum has the following works: *The Fiddler's Lunch, The Swiss Church, Entry to the Port of Sète, Beer Hour.* The museum in Béziers has *The Cooper's Refreshment Stall.*"

The winemaker closed the thick volume and took leave of the two women with the courteous deference that spoke of his traditional upbringing and good British manners. When he left the workshop, he crossed the Place Saint-Michel and bought a lamb kebab from a tiny take-out. Then he went to sit at the base of the bell tower facing the church.

Around him, a group of acne-faced teenagers were playing with a soft-drink can. Another group of young Kabyles from northern Algeria was shooting hoops on an outdoor court near the Gothic bell tower. On the steps in front of the church, a couple of lovers whispered to each other. Nobody paid any attention to Benjamin Cooker. The sun was warm, and no heads turned to see him savor his too-fatty, too-spicy overcooked sandwich that should have ended up in the first garbage can he found.

5

Dark clouds swept in with the tide change in the early afternoon, and a light, damp wind began to blow. The shrieking of the seagulls dissipated along the docks, a reminder that the ocean lapped right up to the city gates.

Before returning to Grangebelle, where he hoped to work on his manuscript, Benjamin Cooker made a detour to the Moniales Haut-Brion. He found Virgile busy in the cellars with two of the estate's workers. The contaminated barrels had been isolated, and they were preparing to decant them into stainless steel tanks. The winemaker's visit was not particularly appreciated when he announced that two other barrels needed to be set apart as quickly as possible. Alexandrine de la Palussière had left a message on Benjamin's cell phone, indicating the numbers of the barrels in which she had detected worrisome quantities of the yeast.

"The full scope of this hasn't hit me yet," Denis Massepain said with a sigh.

"Keep your spirits up. We will find a solution," Benjamin said. "I can't guarantee that we will save the entire production, but we will limit the damage."

"Six barrels! Do you realize what that means? Six barrels are already ruined."

Benjamin quickly calculated the extent of the disaster. It represented about eighteen hundred bottles, as each barrel held just over fifty-nine gallons. If they didn't find an effective parry, this would be a serious loss for the winery, which had only 12.85 acres of vineyard. He was not the full-time winemaker at this estate, but he knew its ins and outs perfectly. They left nothing to chance here, and the Moniales could have served as an example for any winemaking school. They set their planting density correctly at ninety-five hundred plants per two and a half acres. They grew grape varieties that corresponded to the *Appellation d'Origine Contrôlée* for Pessac-Léognan, with forty percent merlot, fifteen percent cabernet franc, and forty-five percent cabernet sauvignon. The average age of the vines was thirty years. They neglected none of the necessary steps in caring for the vines' development, with experienced personnel removing shoots, pruning buds, and thinning out leaves and plants. Hand harvesting meant that each parcel got the greatest care. Each batch spent a reasonable period of fifteen to twenty-four days in tanks. Barrel aging lasted around eighteen months, favoring the most traditional malolactic fermentation. And nobody could reproach sanitation on the premises.

"I just can't figure out what's gone wrong. This is very strange indeed," Benjamin said.

"What can we do?" Denis asked, running a nervous hand through his hair.

"Okay, so we have three new barrels and three others dating from last year. Is that correct?"

"Yes, you know that I renew half of the barrels each year. That is exactly what I can't explain. It can't come from the wood!"

"I know your supplier. He produces superior barrels. My secretary called the cooperage, and they checked their orders and delivery dates. None of the other estates have had any problems. But I don't agree that it doesn't come from the wood."

"Why? What's your idea?"

"Wood is the only vector that facilitates such a quick contamination. You know as well as I do that it harbors and protects all kinds of contaminants. One slip in monitoring or a sulfur dioxide addition that's a little shy and…"

"Let me stop you right there," Denis Massepain interrupted. "If the wood were contaminated, it would not be limited to a specific number of barrels. The whole production would be polluted, if only because of handling and the cross-use of cellar equipment."

"Virgile!" Benjamin shouted in the direction of the fermenting room. "Come here. I need to ask you something."

The assistant appeared without delay, his face sweating.

"Can you decant the six barrels?"

"Right now?" the assistant asked, a little taken aback.

"Why? Are you in some hurry? Do you have a date?"

"No, sir, but, uh, that could take some time. We won't finish before the middle of the night."

"In this line of work, you need to know how to stay up late, young man. And now you are going to experience your first night nursing the sick."

"I can ask my two workers to stay," said the owner. "And I'll change, because I think we'll need at least four people."

So Denis Massepain returned to the manor house to change out of his city clothes, and Benjamin took his assistant aside to talk to him quietly. He reviewed each of the steps involved in decanting the barrels and asked Virgile to make sure he eliminated the lees and deposits, to do it in a sheltered place, and to reference the metal tanks using the barrel numbers. He also asked that each of the empty barrels be set outside the cellar and covered with tarps.

"Do you have any questions?" the winemaker asked, looking at his watch.

Virgile promised that he would follow his instructions exactly and reminded Benjamin that it was a bad time to take the beltway or the main streets. He would end up stuck in traffic with everyone coming home from work.

"You're right," Benjamin said, making a face. "I had better not return to Médoc right away. I'll drop in on someone who is not expecting me."

§ § §

Dr. Pierre Baldès had cleverly distributed the folds of his shirt in a vain attempt to hide a slight paunch. He had a plain elegance found in men who have been established for some time and a certain bearing despite his growing portliness and skin exposed too often to the sun. Benjamin nodded a greeting as he entered the office, feeling a little sleepy after spending two hours in the waiting room browsing the mundane gossip in the magazines and listening to annoyed patients snort.

"Please sit down, sir. What can I do for you?" The ENT doctor asked with the particular indifference found in older clinical practitioners.

"Well, I'm quite healthy. My nose is intact, and my palate still alert. I do not have any problems to speak of, Doctor."

The doctor stared at Benjamin, wondering if he was dealing with a joker or someone who was chronically depressed.

"Please excuse me. I have not introduced myself. Benjamin Cooker here. I have come to discuss something that is, well, uh, personal."

"I'm reassured. For a minute there, I thought I had a crazy one on my hands." Pierre Baldès smiled, pinching his lips a little.

"I would like to talk to you about a painting," Benjamin said, getting straight to the point.

"A painting? Correct me if I'm wrong, you are Cooker, from the *Cooker Guide?*"

"Yes, and as it turns out, we both bought the same painting. Well, nearly the same. Let's just say that we have two paintings that look very much the same."

"I don't understand what you are talking about," said the doctor. "We have two paintings that are the same, but they're not really the same? And what work of art are you referring to?"

"A late nineteenth-century overmantel that you had restored on the Rue Notre-Dame. It is a rural scene showing grape harvesting under a blue sky, with a building in the background."

"Yes, I have that painting. And you are telling me that you own the same one or nearly the same one? I am very surprised. It is a rather minor work. Well done, yes, but fairly naive. I do not think that it could have been interesting enough to copy."

"That is what I think, as well," interrupted Benjamin. "And that is why I have come to see you. Would it be too much to ask to have five minutes of your time to see your overmantel? I won't be long. The time of an appointment, no longer."

"An appointment that's not covered by your insurance?" the doctor joked. "In that case, it could end up costing you a lot."

"I don't want to impose on you. I could stop by another day."

"No, not at all. Follow me."

They went through a hidden doorway and climbed the stairs to Baldès's apartment. It was well appointed, elegant but conventional. It looked like a spread in an interior design magazine, with just that touch of originality, that fanciful detail and hint of color acceptable and necessary to justify the decorator's fee.

The overmantel reigned over a white marble fireplace in front of two large purple sofas. The frame had been restored with gold leaf, and the original mirror seemed to be just as mottled as Benjamin's There was no doubt about it. They had been done by the same artist. The same soft light, subdued by dark leafy vegetation, bathed the scene. The rows of vines formed waves descending toward the bottom of the hill, giving an identical perspective, although the people here had their backs to the painter and were harvesting in small groups of two and three. In the distance, it was easy to make out the stout silhouette of the manor house, whose roof could belong to none other than the Haut-Brion château.

"Just what I thought," Benjamin murmured, moving closer to the painting.

"And that is?"

"You see those two square towers on the left and the projection on the right wing, with its two pointed roof turrets? It can be none other than Haut-Brion."

"I confirm," Baldès said in a near whisper, as if he did not want to disturb the winemaker's thoughts.

"That is a very fine surprise. Very fine, indeed! I own your painting's twin, except that mine represents Mission Haut-Brion."

"And it is a harvest scene, as well?" the doctor asked.

"With just a few minor differences. It has the same perspective, the same tones, the same characters, and the same trees. I have a snapshot from before it was cleaned and restored."

Benjamin stepped back a couple of feet and took out the picture that Pascale Dartigeas had lent him. He closed one eye and held it at arm's length toward the overmantel.

"Yes, I'm under the impression that these two painting belong together, Dr. Baldès. Look closely. Yours is on the right, and the trees on the left side fit perfectly with the trees on mine."

The doctor took the photograph and lifted it to see it in perspective. He half-closed his left eye and looked perplexed.

"Focus on the left side of the painting," Benjamin advised. "After awhile, it will jump out at you."

"You're right. The two scenes go together. It's incredible. There is a perfect continuity between the poplar trees, the cloud, the little pond, and the rows of grapevines."

"Do you know where yours came from?" Benjamin asked.

"I bought it from an antique dealer in Maynac. For next to nothing, I must admit. But the restoration cost me quite a bit."

"I found mine in Blaye. The price was not particularly excessive either, but quite a bit of restoration work is needed to fix some serious tears and fly specks, and the sky needs touching up."

"They must have been stored under terrible conditions."

"I have to admit that I am curious about where they came from."

"Probably a local château or some bourgeois home. You'll need to ask an art specialist or historian. I know of only one person who could tell you, if he were willing to talk to you."

"And where would I find him?"

"In Pessac. His name is Ferdinand Ténotier, and he lives in the Cité Frugès. He's easy to find, and you can't mistake him. A strange fellow, but he has a brilliant mind. He used to teach at the university, which apparently fired him over some serious issue. He's been retired for as long as I've known him, and there is no telling how old he is."

"A historian?" Benjamin asked.

"Better than that. He has no specialty but is an expert in everything. You can always try to see him, but I wish you luck with that."

Before taking his leave, Benjamin offered to buy the doctor's overmantel, making it clear that he was willing to pay a nice sum for it. The doctor gave an evasive and polite response.

"Perhaps," he said. "I'll have to think about it."

Benjamin could tell from Pierre Baldès's tone that he would never sell his painting. He hid his disappointment and agreed to autograph a copy of the latest edition of the *Cooker Guide,* which the doctor had on his shelf.

6

Benjamin Cooker drove slowly through the town
of Pessac and then parked his convertible in the
shade of a scraggly pine tree. It did not take him
long to find the old Ferdinand Ténotier in the
Cité Frugès, a working-class neighborhood designed in 1925 by Le Corbusier at the request of
industrialist Henri Frugès. The homes were made
of reinforced concrete and had angular facades
and suspended decks. A few had been renovated
over the years, their original blue and green hues
covered up. On the whole, however, the modernist
garden housing development was a chaotic landscape, with blocks of eroded buildings emerging
from sickly vegetation.

When Benjamin asked where he could find
Ténotier, some people tensed up, while others
joked. All agreed that the former professor was
crazy and dangerous. He lived at 12 Rue Le
Corbusier, in a ramshackle building where the
dreams of the great visionary architect were
showing a number of cracks. Benjamin planted

himself in front of the structure and observed the leprous walls, the original wooden shutters all askew, the rusted drainpipes, sheet-metal roofing that was falling in on one side, and the large patches of mold that marbled the gray cement.

He knocked several times before a red, somewhat bitter-looking face deigned to appear in the half-open doorway. Benjamin Cooker introduced himself, smiling pleasantly and saying his name in a clear voice that didn't seem overly ingratiating.

"I know who you are," the man said curtly.

"Thank you for seeing me. I need your insight, Mr. Ténotier. I was told that you are the only..."

"Who's talking about me?"

The interview was going to be touch and go. The man was suspicious, but Benjamin had expected this. Ténotier had an extremely piercing look and poor teeth behind thin lips. He had gone several days without shaving. His greasy hair hung under the collar of a grimy shirt. He had neglected his nails. His nose was spongy, his cheeks hollow and full of blotches. His back was hunched, and his breath was bad enough to asphyxiate a herd of buffaloes. He reeked of solitude and hatred, intelligence and abandonment. A man to avoid.

"Dr. Pierre Baldès told me that you most certainly could..."

"That one still thinks about me, does he?"

"He had nothing but good to say about you."

"Compliments are cheap."

"I assure you…"

"Will it take long?" the old man spit out in a wine-dripped hiccup.

"I'll be quick, no more than a quarter of an hour," Benjamin said with a composure he often called upon in prickly situations.

"In that case," Ténotier grumbled, disappearing to let the winemaker pass.

As soon as Benjamin entered the main room, a violent smell of ammonia stung his throat and nose. A cat brushed between his legs, followed by two others, and then came a whole drove of raw-boned felines he could vaguely make out in the darkness. A shredded blanket covered a picture window, and weak rays of light filtered through the torn fabric.

"Sit down," Ténotier muttered, pointing to a chair where a tabby, as scrawny as all the others, was sleeping.

Benjamin preferred to sit on a heavily clawed stool. The old man set two sturdy glasses down on the table, grabbed a cardboard pack and poured some red wine.

"We'll drink together. I'm sure it's been quite some time since you tasted a wine like this one," Ténotier threw out, with a hint of provocation in his raspy voice.

Without letting himself be disconcerted, Benjamin lifted the glass to his lips and swallowed a mouthful of revolting plonk that burned his throat.

"That's true. It has been a long time," he said, making a face.

"Everything is going to hell! I drink something that doesn't deserve to be called wine from square packs and cardboard kegs. I drink shit because I'm poor, sir, but I'm not ashamed to be poor. I'm only ashamed of the times we live in, of what people throw to guys like me. I'm ashamed that people actually dare to sell crap like this on the pretext that others like me can't afford anything else. It's shit, I'm telling you!"

Despite his advanced state of alcoholism, his dirty fingernails, and the havoc and feverishness on his face, Ferdinand Ténotier had a lyrical disillusionment like that of a wise man who had probed humanity until he reached self-disgust and hatred. He seemed precipitously near the end of his rope.

"This is the first time I've been here. I had no idea that the development was so spread out," Benjamin noted, thinking it best to change the subject.

"It's a ghost town, a concrete cemetery. That's what it has become! And the middle classes get off on moving into a historical area. It's all being bought up by architects, doctors, lawyers—people who think they know something. They invest in cultural heritage. Some heritage. Just junk!"

"It is a surprising place, though. Have you lived here for a long time?"

"Fifty years. A little more even. My parents lived here before me. They were real working-class people. Good people. Nothing in their heads, but huge hearts. We're all screwed. The working class is all gone."

Ferdinand Ténotier downed his glass in one shot and poured himself another, a lost look in his eyes, his head down.

"It was a pioneering idea in the nineteen twenties," Benjamin said. "This concrete housing development with large picture windows, private bathrooms, and gardens."

He regretted his words as soon as they came out. The old man threw him a ferocious look and spilled his wine on his shirtsleeve.

"Le Corbusier was just a bunch of theories. He was an ideological con artist, a communist asshole who sold his body to patrons to build dumps for the proletariat. I shit on those illusionists who preached social justice, humankind and all that crap, who filled their pockets until they burst. And above all, sir, they continue to sermonize, to give us lessons about how to live.

"Mediocrity killed off all the real thinkers. Nobody ever listens to people who really think, because thinking is harmful. You understand, nobody will lend an ear to anyone who says what we really are and where we are really headed. We should blow up all the universities and schools where they don't even know how to speak Latin anymore, where everyone thinks that Roland Garros was a tennis player. They harbor soft asses, ignoramuses, little neat and clean people, career-minded shit eaters who will go on strike only when it doesn't interfere with their schedules and their vacation leave. They want to pretend to carry out a revolution, but only if it doesn't threaten their mortgages, their lawnmowers, and their savings accounts. They are dying of comfort, with empty heads and full stomachs.

"Le Corbusier loved glory, medals, and money. The bastard hated the people. He knew nothing about the little people. Because they stink, they smell of sweat, they shit out kids by the truckload, they use bad words, the people! Mind you, Le Corbusier had at least one thing going for him, his first name was Charles Edouard, and that no-body could take away from him. He had a very French first name, a small saving grace."

He drank two glasses of wine, one after the other, wiped off his mustache with the back of his hand, and stared at his visitor. His eyes were bright, very black, and it was impossible to make out the pupils.

"Why are you here?" he asked, rubbing his stubble-covered cheeks.

Benjamin took out the picture of his overmantel and gave it to the old man, who slid it under a ray of warm light.

"Ah, you too," Ténotier chuckled.

"You certainly know that Pierre Baldès has a similar painting. I guess he also came to see you."

"Yes, he came, and he refused to drink my poison. Spineless!"

Benjamin took this as a compliment.

"Come on, let's drink to all those delicate doctors! Bottoms up! Raise your glass to all those savant monkeys who can't read Hippocrates in the original." Ferdinand burped and filled up his glass.

He loudly clinked Benjamin's glass.

"Your painting is Mission Haut-Brion. The doc's represents the Château de Haut-Brion. I have nothing else to tell you."

"That I knew already," Benjamin said, without showing any impatience. "But what is most astonishing is that they go together. The right side of my painting joins up perfectly with the left side of Baldès's. They must be part of a two-paneled work made for some sort of mural."

"Probably," grumbled Ferdinand.

"And I am curious to know where they come from, since the theme is rather rare."

"Your lousy paintings aren't famous. They're hackwork."

"I think they are rather well done for that kind of painting," Benjamin said. "A little naive, yes, and rather broadly drawn, but they are not lacking in character. And the lighting is well mastered, particularly where the sky meets the trees. They have a nice brushstroke to them."

"Well, sir, I believe that everyone should be held accountable for his own taste. Only the spineless say the contrary. But I don't have time to waste on two worthless sketches just because they were painted locally."

Benjamin caught the reference as it flew by.

"You are sure that these works were painted by an artist in the region? Perhaps a painter from Pessac?"

"When the doc came to see me, he brought his painting, and I admit I had the feeling I had seen it somewhere before. But at the time, I couldn't for the life of me remember where."

"And has it come back to you since?" the winemaker asked, trying not to look too insistent.

"I think so."

Ferdinand Ténotier filled up their glasses again. He threw the empty cardboard carton to the back of the room and leaned over to grab another one from the floor.

"These overmantels were in the reading room at the Château de Vallon," the old man said. "I saw them at the beginning of the nineteen fifties, when they were still hanging above the fireplace, which was made of Pyrenees marble."

"The Château de Vallon?" the winemaker said, surprised. "I seem to recall seeing a label with that name on it on an old bottle."

"If you still have that bottle, guard it with vigilance. It's a relic!"

"I don't have it in my wine cellar, but I certainly saw it at an auction or something like that."

"Those damned urban planners made their way through there!" barked the old man. "The Château de Vallon was totally destroyed in 1966, and you'll find a housing project where it stood. Isn't the republic a beautiful thing! Always ready to trash what belongs to us! The châteaux in Pessac that have been torn down in recent years all belonged to us, to you, to me, to everyone! We all own our history! The people of France. I tell you, it all belongs to the people of France! What a wretched shame. A handsome château like Vallon. It was built in 1777 by Victor Louis, the same architect who built Bordeaux's Grand Théâtre. It had a sloping roof, a large flight of stairs, huge grounds, and then there were the vineyards. Several acres that produced a fine red Graves. If my memory still serves me, I believe it got a silver medal at the Bordeaux fair in 1895."

"I can check my archives, if you're interested," Benjamin offered.

"You want archives. I'll show you some you'll never see again."

Ténotier had trouble standing up, then staggered to the greasy buffet and brought back a shoebox full of sepia-colored photographs and ancient postcards. He hands trembled.

"Look at that! Château Fanning-Lafontaine, torn down in 1980. The grounds were remarkable, with rare tree species, including some Louisiana cypress that the Baron Sarget imported. There were acres and acres of vineyards right next to the Haut-Brion estates. There was a workers clinic there before it got sold off. If you go there now, you'll find a housing development. Here, this is a picture of the Château Condom, which belonged to Dr. Azam, the father-in-law of the great historian Camille Jullian. Another housing development. In 1921! They drew a road right through the middle of the estate, right there where you see the orange trees. It's sickening. What a waste!"

He gulped another glass of wine as he continued to go through his documents. His commentary became harsher and harsher. There was sadness mixed with violence in the pathetic drunk's voice. Benjamin couldn't help feeling something himself in seeing these images of a time that had already been forgotten, lost in gravel and cement blocks. The Château Monbalon, an estate that spread over one hundred and twenty acres, including twelve with vineyards, five with prairies, five more that were farmed, and eighty-nine with pinewood forest and private hunting grounds. There, in 1927, the Mirante housing development grew up like a wart, before the château itself was destroyed in 1982 because it had fallen into disrepair. The same thing happened to the Domaine de Macédo and the Château Haut-Bourgailh. Just like the great estate of Haut-Livrac, one of the oldest noble homes in Pessac, which produced fifteen barrels of fine wine annually before urbanization devoured it. The same destiny was reserved for the Château Haut-Lévêque and its six barrels of red wine, the Château Bersol and its fifteen barrels, and Château Halloran, which produced twenty-six barrels of well-structured wine before being turned into a hospital. All these elegant monuments, surrounded by landscaped grounds and domesticated vines, disappeared at the dawn of the 1960s to create an industrial zone.

Ténotier had a few words, a date, a reminder, a legend, a political allusion, a sharp comment, or a mean statement to make for each photo. This man's bad-mouthing and his endless knowledge began to seduce Benjamin, who enjoyed listening to the point of sipping his cheap wine without balking.

"Here is a postcard I always have a hard time looking at," the old man continued. "The Château Saige-Formanoir pissed out fifteen or so tanks of red wine at the end of the nineteenth century, and then the fifteen acres of vineyards were pulled out in 1956, the same year the Garonne River froze over. That was the beginning of the end. Starting in 1970, they built eight eighteen-story buildings on the estate. All that so that four thousand idiots could have hot water, an elevator, a tiny balcony, and the opportunity to hear their neighbors fart.

"But the worst was the university, with its thirty thousand students who arrived in 1979. Are there really thirty thousand kids capable of reasoning and writing a dissertation without any spelling mistakes? Do we really need all those fact-stuffed brains to keep the country going? They tore down the Château de Rocquencourt to set up a sports complex on the campus: nearly six hundred and twenty acres of intellectual desert for brats who buy soft drinks and don't give a shit that it wrecked acres of vineyards!"

There was already a serious dent in the second carton of wine when old Ferdinand began telling the story of the Haut-Brion domaine. Of course, Benjamin knew the basic outline, as he had become interested in this exceptional spot very early on, but he was dumbfounded by the fallen professor's encyclopedic knowledge; the institution must have judged him as disreputable as he was cumbersome. Ténotier was a smooth drunk. His hesitating elocution and crimson face showed his fatigue, but he babbled with panache and made theatrical gestures as if inspired. His presentation was littered with anecdotes, details, dynastic

successions, historical perspectives, religious refer-
ences, risqué episodes, obscure testimonials, legal
cases, pertinent trade analyses, climate vagaries,
and vintages.

"Do you know *The Pessac March*? The Saint-
Orens family wrote the song, the music by the
father and the words by the son. A fine piece of
idiocy," he shouted out as he began to sing with
all his heart.

> Pessac, jewel of the 'burbs,
> Making Bordeaux ever more superb,
> Eastward, on for some miles,
> Can be seen its gleaming roof tiles.
> All around its aging church
> And the old town's ancient birch
> Dressed with pretty, stylish flowers
> Are rising practical, modern towers.

His voice was quaking, both fluty and hoarse.
He caught his breath between two stanzas.

> Both farmers and winemaker manors
> Pushed away by town planners
> As outward grew the city,
> With no nostalgia and no pity.
> Yet Pessac held tight in its bosom
> A gem worthy of its wisdom,
> That source of ever-grand wine,
> Moniales Haut-Brion and its vine.

The last note was prolonged, suspended in the air of sour wine.

"And it goes on like that for eight verses. Those were the days," he said, looking into the distance. "Today, if you want to dabble in bagpipes, you have to confine yourself to the Pessac Accordion Club in a concrete music school. You'll never make good musicians by locking them up in an old factory. They need to breathe, to fill their lungs. There's also the Pessac ditty by Edouard Trouilh. The melody is not very complicated, only one flat in the key.

He blew his nose into his fingers, cleared his throat, and began to hum an approximate melody.

Two things keep me alive,
The only reasons I survive,
Haut-Brion and my Belle
Nothing could be so swell,
One for its drunken charms,
The other to hold in my arms.

"It's all bunk, trivial, but it was a time when you could still sing after a meal without being considered an idiot. The girls were trusting, and the boys as voracious as they are today, but things were less formal. There used to be education in this country, before we lost the colonies. Education is very important, Mr. Cooker. It has nothing to do with breeding. You are an educated man. It shows.

You are capable of putting up with a washed-up old man like me for more than an hour, and you are not just pretending to listen. I could almost end up liking you, if I still believed in people."

Benjamin remained silent. The old man's cheap wine had started to go to his head and upset his stomach.

§ § §

"I'm going to tell you something, Mr. Cooker," Ferdinand muttered, his voice pasty with alcohol.

"Your two overmantels, well, the truth is, there were three of them."

Benjamin's eyes widened.

"You mean it was a triptych?"

"Yes, three panels. Not one more, not one less. You weren't expecting that, were you?"

"And the other painting completes the scene, I suppose?"

"Evidently. And the solution, well, you'll find it in water. For once, that will be a change for you."

"In water? What do you mean?"

"Today, Mr. Cooker, you shouldn't invest in wine. If you want to become rich and hold everyone by the short hairs, sell water. Soon enough, you'll have to beg to get a cup of water, and when it comes to that, well, we're on our way out! Water's a gift from God! It's all going to hell, I tell you. It's all going to hell!"

Ferdinand Ténotier yawned, belched several times, and placed his hands flat on the greasy wine-stained table. A black and white cat jumped up and rubbed against his right cheek. The old man swiped at it, sending it to the other side of the room. Then he placed his purple face on his crossed arms and fell asleep.

7

A cement truck rumbled in the distance, downing out the birds that were nesting in the trees. As Benjamin walked across the grounds, he looked to the top of the century-old cedar tree, where a turtledove was grooming its feathers. He followed the thin flow of water in the Peugue. The creek slowly made its way between patches of herbs and around large roots that had grown out of the ground, blocking its passage and forcing it to make detours.

Benjamin Cooker was exhausted after his meeting in the Cité Frugès. The old Ténotier's awful cheap wine had left his mouth cottony. The smell of cat piss was still stinging his nostrils, and after spending so much time in the shadows, he had to keep blinking his eyes. Those two hours were enough to wipe out a tasting career and compromise his reputation as a winemaker. People were busy at work near the Moniales Haut-Brion cellars, which quickly brought him back to reality. He greeted the assembled crowd from a distance so as not to burn himself in the steam coming out of the barrels. They had started washing the contaminated casks early that morning. Virgile left the team to pursue the work while he reported to his boss.

"Everything went perfectly, sir. We finished decanting around one this morning. We attacked disinfecting at seven, and we should be finished soon."

"Is everyone following the instructions?" Benjamin asked without showing concern for his assistant's fatigue.

The young man was clearly strong and well built, spoiled by nature even, yet his face was pale and wrinkled from the lack of sleep. He had deep purple bags under his eyes.

"I followed your instructions closely," the assistant said. "I added the same amount of ozone to each barrel, and I raised the water temperature to two hundred degrees."

"Did you use constant pressure?"

"Yes, but then I prolonged the treatment time and spent a quarter of an hour on each barrel. I think that should do it."

"You still have to be wary of ozone. It's an effective disinfectant, but it causes oxidation that could promote certain volatile substances that influence the wine's aroma and the wood's quality."

"We rinsed at high pressure, sir. Long enough. I really followed your recommendations to the letter."

"Very good, then. Don't change anything," Benjamin said, waving at Denis Massepain, who was walking toward them from the château.

The assistant disappeared into the thick white steam rising from the barrels being rinsed with the high-pressure stream of hot water. Virgile was demonstrating a lot of energy and concentration. He was also showing a natural authority that allowed him to give orders to the workers without being arrogant.

"Your new employee seems quite good," Denis said, giving Benjamin a tired handshake.

"Yes, he's a good recruit. He works hard and keeps smiling. Those are two qualities that are hard to find these days."

"Is everything okay, Benjamin?"

"I think so. We'll proceed with sulfiting tomorrow. Doing it today would have been ideal, but my lab manager has to finish something urgent and cannot make it earlier."

"Did you tell her?" Denis asked with a worried look. "Does she really need to be here?"

"I had to. But you have nothing to fear. Alexandrine de la Palussière can be trusted. I need her here to adapt the sulfur dioxide dosage. She is the one who recommended that we use ozone to clean the barrels, and I think it's the best technique. Chlorine could accelerate the formation of trichlorophenol, which would then break down into trichloroanisole. Don't ask me for the specifics. I don't know anything more, but from experience, I can guarantee that we will avoid any moldy aromas this way. And it's better to forget any chemical detergents and fungicides, such as quaternary ammonium compound, because they always leave a residue after rinsing."

"I'll leave it up to you. I don't have a choice, do I?" sighed Massepain. "I haven't slept since this whole thing began, and I prefer not to say too much about it to Thérèse. She worries enough as it is."

"You're right. The best thing to do for now is to stand by your team and wait until the end of next week. I think that in a few days I'll be able to tell you where things stand."

Benjamin and his friend took a short walk on the grounds, making small talk that was not entirely futile. It relaxed Massepain a bit. And the winemaker took advantage of the moment to get a closer look at the new cabernet franc stock that had just been planted on a small parcel. Tender sprouts were starting to bud; they would not give clusters for another two or three years. He glanced over the meticulous rows of vines, quickly judging the state of the soil composed of thick Gunz gravel, sand, and clay and noted with pleasure that the vineyards had just been plowed. His eyes stopped for a moment on the Haut-Brion estate hilltop that dominated the neighborhood. Then he cupped his hands around his mouth and called out to his assistant. "Are you almost finished? We're off in five minutes, Virgile!"

§ § §

The two men dropped the newest samples at the lab and by some miracle found a parking spot between two construction-site fences near the Place de la Bourse. Then they walked up the Cours du Chapeau Rouge, passing the Grand Théâtre's massive columns and then turning on the Allée de Tourny to reach Noailles. Benjamin had the near-daily habit of lunching at this elegant brasserie, where he was greeted with somewhat affected nods from Bordeaux citizens of note, although they never dared to disturb him.

The table for the esteemed Mr. Cooker had been held for him, as usual, and the two men were welcomed with the polite friendliness given to long-time regulars. They were ravenous and opted for two quick starters followed by grilled fish served with a dry Pessac-Léognan white. Benjamin let his assistant choose the wine, which took quite some time, as he hesitated between a

Château Carbonnieux and a Château Ferran before finally deciding on a 1998 Château Latour-Martillac.

"You deserve it, Virgile!"

"I have to admit that there's no time to get bored with you!"

They talked about this and that, trivial things and insignificant memories that were nonetheless important, because the two of them were getting to know each other. At the end of the meal, Benjamin offered the young man a cigar, but he declined politely in favor of an espresso. Then the winemaker suggested a digestive walk under the Jardin Public's blue cedar trees. Before going to the park, Virgile asked to stop at his studio apartment on the Rue Saint-Rémi, so they made a quick detour along the top of the Rue Sainte-Catherine. Benjamin waited outside, and his assistant came back down quickly, holding a large plastic bag.

"What are lugging around in that sack?" Benjamin asked.

"Stale bread. I keep it to feed the ducks and the fish in the park."

"Do you do that a lot?"

"I'm a country boy, and where I come from, nothing goes to waste. I can't get myself to throw bread away."

"I feel twenty years younger in your company, my dear Virgile," Benjamin said, clearly moved.

"I often brought my daughter to the park, and every time, we had our stash of stale bread."

"I didn't know you had a daughter."

"Ah, Virgile, if you only knew Margaux. She is pretty as a picture, twenty-four years old and now living in New York."

"What is she doing there?"

"She is in the import-export business, specializing in regional products."

Benjamin said nothing more on the subject. He didn't like his life to be an open book, and he made it a habit to never give himself away in the first chapters. Virgile asked no other questions, and they walked in silence to the gilded gates opening onto the public park's bouquet of trees.

Gravel crunched under their heels. They passed a bronze bust of the French writer François Mauriac, sculpted by the Russian-born artist Ossip Zadkine. The sculptor had given the writer an eagle's profile, high cheekbones, a sharply carved chin, an excessively hollowed neck, and the face of a mystic ascetic, showing a deep understanding of the Malaga writer's dual nature. At the end of the central walkway, they passed the small Guérin family puppet-show stage. Its wooden shutters were closed. They stopped on a metal footbridge that crossed over one of the branches of the large pond.

"When I was a kid, I was scared to death of falling in among the carp," Benjamin said, looking dreamily at the water. "Later, I was even more frightened when Margaux leaned over the railing."

"Well, it is teeming with fish!" Virgile said, tossing in some stale crumbs.

Hundreds of fish rose to the surface in a single movement and then launched into a violent combat. Benjamin and Virgile observed this sticky carpet of open jaws, bulging eyes and knife-like fins with distaste. The carp made a ghoulish clicking sound as they swallowed the pieces of bread. Some ducks tried their luck in the fray, in vain. They floundered in the whirlpool of viscous scales without managing to collect anything but the crumbs of the feast.

The two men then crossed the playground to reach the other part of the pond, where they spread out breadcrumbs for the numerous sparrows that nested near the spillway. Two blond mothers appeared on a walkway. They had the elegant air of the well bred from the Quinconces neighborhood. But their desperate shouts contradicted their sophisticated looks. "Jean-Baptiste! Eugénie!" they yelled as they peered into the bushes and scanned the flowerbeds.

A uniformed park officer with a wild mustache joined them and also started looking through the bushes. Other mothers in straight dark-blue skirts and white blouses joined the search, as well, followed by a stream of children in English-style clothing. There was something terribly chic about the chaos.

"Can I be frank with you?" Virgile asked suddenly as he scattered crumbs on the grass.

"I don't expect anything less of you," Benjamin answered.

"Well, okay, uh, I really think that, well, you might think I'm paranoid, but this spoilage thing, it just doesn't make sense. Not in an estate like Moniales Haut-Brion. Particularly Brettanomyces. Especially not in a cellar that is maintained so well. I've been hanging around with the team for a few days now, and I assure you, they are very serious."

"I know," Benjamin said.

"And Denis Massepain knows the business. He doesn't let anything get by him and has an eye on everything. He's a real winemaker, and I don't see how he could have let a contamination of this scope happen."

"I agree."

"As far as I'm concerned, there is only one possibility, but it's hard to voice such a thing."

"Go ahead, Virgile. Don't beat around the bush. Say what you have to say."

"Someone had to slip those spores into the barrels," the assistant said, tossing a small slice of bread to a turkey with a low-hanging wattle. "I've thought it over and over, and I can't think of any other possibility."

"You are not alone. I've been thinking that for a while now."

"Do you know if he has any enemies? Someone who is angry enough to ruin his life?"

"Not to my knowledge. Denis is loyal, calm, and correct. But I am not a good judge. He's my friend."

"Who knows? Maybe something happened with a member of his staff?"

"His workers and cellar master have been there for years, and the atmosphere at the estate is relatively serene. He is surrounded by motivated people. No, I doubt it's an inside job."

"Maybe one of his competitors wants to throw him off balance? Someone who is jealous and wants to cast a shadow on the estate? Someone full of envy who wants to put him on his knees?"

Benjamin took the final chunk of bread from the bottom of the plastic bag and threw it near a swan, which barely stretched its neck before continuing on its way with disdain.

"If the profession had to resolve its differences with biological warfare, where would we be, my dear Virgile? You know the wine world. It's a milieu where people observe and watch each other, sometimes with fear but always with respect, and everyone knows how to recognize his colleagues' value. Estate owners even help each other to a certain extent. You have to admit that the professional groups set up for each appellation bring the harvesters together and make them stronger. Or at least that is what we all pretend to believe! When there are hostile feelings, they play out in the trading halls. Nobody gives any gifts when it comes to selling one's stock. But everyone is always courteous. May the best man win!"

"I want to believe you, but I am convinced that there is someone around the Moniales who visited the cellar and who knows perfectly well how to taint a barrel of wine. I don't know how he managed, but he knows the premises and how to get in. There must not be that many people who have the keys and know the alarm code. Denis Massepain is the only one who can tell us for sure."

The two worried mothers had wound up finding their children. A crowd had formed around a bush where the little Jean-Baptiste and Eugénie were hiding, trying to strangle a mallard.

"Your reasoning is sound," Benjamin said. "Have you read Montesquieu?"

"No, I haven't read any Montesquieu, nor have I touched Montaigne, and I never finished a single book by Mauriac. I've done none of the local writers. I guess I should be a little ashamed, living in Bordeaux and all."

"Mostly, it's too bad," Benjamin said.

"And what does he have to say, your Montesquieu?"

"If my memory serves me, he says, 'I prefer the company of peasants, because they have not been educated sufficiently to reason incorrectly.'"

8

Virgile steered the car with his left hand and scratched his head with his right. He looked pre-occupied. His lips were pursed, and his eyebrows were knotted.

"That Montesquieu wrote some bullshit."

"Who hasn't?" Benjamin sighed.

"I remember one of my French teachers telling a not-so-glorious story about him."

"Is that so?"

"In one of his books he wrote that King François I had refused gifts offered by Christopher Columbus, but François I wasn't even born when Columbus discovered America!"

"Just goes to show you, my dear Virgile, that you should always check your sources. That said, I've always been suspicious of the philosopher. In fact, Montesquieu seriously gets on my nerves. I shouldn't tell you that, because in this town it is not seemly to criticize local heroes, particular-ly when that glory reaches beyond the nearby Libourne hills."

"Mum's the word, I promise!" Virgile smiled.

"Lesson givers have always exasperated me. Montesquieu spread all kinds of holier-than-thou theories about slavery, none of which kept him from stuffing himself when Bordeaux's slave traders invited him over. The world is filled with moralizers who forget to sweep in front of their own doors. Are you interested in history? You know, in those things that often bore young people your age?"

"When you're born in Bergerac, you can't escape the past. Take my word for it," Virgile responded. "I've always found it fascinating, but sometimes I feel crushed by all those old stones and a little overshadowed by the illustrious dead and memories of grand battles."

"Battles that had no reason for being," added Benjamin. "But we have to know about them to keep history from repeating itself. Yesterday, I met an amazing fellow. One day I'll take you to see him. If you like the little stories that make up the big picture of history, you'll spend an enriching, albeit slightly frightening, time with him."

Benjamin told Virgile about Ferdinand Ténotier, sparing no detail, including the overpowering cat smell, the cheap wine, the sorry state of the apartment, the singular atmosphere that reigned in the small Cité Frugès streets, the postcards, and the terribly destiny of Pessac's châteaux. Virgile listened carefully, and the drive seemed short, despite the traffic on the boulevards and the inevitable bottleneck as they neared the Barrière de Pessac intersection. He asked a few questions about Le Corbusier, whose name he vaguely recognized, although he had never seen any of his work. Benjamin offered an explanation that he tried to make impartial, without any value judgments. The young man would have to make up his own mind, and the winemaker did not want to influence him, as he admittedly was no authority in the area of architecture. Le Corbusier had left his mark in the Aquitaine region, from the first experimental houses he built in Lège-Cap-Ferret in 1923 to the futurist buildings constructed in Pessac two years later. Benjamin did not feel especially moved by these structures, but their innovative spirit deserved respect.

During this meandering discussion, Virgile learned of his employer's passion for antiques and painting. The assistant became all the more attentive when Benjamin brought up the two paintings of the Château Haut-Brion and the Mission Haut-Brion, especially when he mentioned the mysterious third painting. The young man did not comment, though. He finally admitted that he didn't know exactly what an overmantel was. Benjamin was happy to explain.

"It's a painting or a decorative panel. At the beginning of the seventeenth century, these panels were often set in moldings and had mirrors.

Overmantel used to refer to the decorative wood-work that complemented the artwork, but now it has come to mean the entire piece, which often hangs over a fireplace. Painted canvases most often have a frame with a small mirror underneath. In French, it's called a *trumeau*, which comes from the old French *trumel*, which meant leg fat or, for a butcher, a beef shank. The word evolved to mean the part of the wall between two windows."

"That's wild," Virgile said. "You could make a fortune on game shows!"

Benjamin smiled and asked him to slow down when they entered Pessac. They crept along the Avenue Jean-Jaurès, a ribbon of pavement bordered on both sides by waves of vineyards whose undulating movement broke the monotony of the suburbs.

"Turn at the next gate to your right," Benjamin said.

"Are we going to…"

"Yes, we are," Benjamin said, suddenly curt.

Virgile skillfully maneuvered the car and drove slowly under a brown stone archway, stopping in the shadow of Château Haut-Brion. Still gripping the steering wheel, he looked up, awestruck at finding himself in the heart of an estate whose prestige had long been the thing of dreams. Benjamin was barely out of the car when a tall, thin man who was wearing a twill suit and appeared to be in his forties greeted him with notable respect. Benjamin asked if it was possible to disturb the steward.

"I am sorry, Mr. Cooker. He is absent, but you are always welcome at Haut-Brion. Is there anything I can do for you?"

"I won't be long. I just need to make a topographical check for the next edition of the guide, and I need to take some notes from the top of the plateau."

"Would you like me to accompany you?"

"Thank you. That will not be necessary, I know the way."

The winemaker and his assistant took off on foot amid the rows of grapevines, climbing the hump of greenery without saying a word. It would have been like being in the countryside, were it not for the incessant dull humming from the north. It sounded like a distant storm brewing in the heat, but in reality it was the barely muffled sound of Bordeaux, mixed with the peripheral grumblings that spread across the suburbs.

They reached the top of the hill in no time. Benjamin caught his breath while he scanned the urban landscape that extended below. He knew immediately that his intuition was correct and that he had finally found what the old Ténotier was referring to. Why hadn't he figured it out sooner? Virgile registered his employer's satisfied nod of recognition without understanding what was going on.

"Of course," Benjamin muttered. "It jumps out at you!"

He approached the water tower that stood in the middle of the Haut-Brion estate, an enormous concrete wart planted right in the vineyards, like a constant reminder that here nature was on shaky ground, barely accepted and on borrowed time. Benjamin looked up. It was not so much the structure's ugliness that caused him to despair, but all those cubic meters of water standing over one of the most prestigious wines in the world, like a vulgar form of provocation.

"This is the water the old man was talking about!" the winemaker said, touching the tower's roughcast.

He took out the picture of his overmantel and looked toward Mission Haut-Brion dozing at the foot of the hillock. It was all there: the dormer windows in the slate roof, the chapel with its stone cross, the two columns at the front gate, the barn transformed into a cellar flanking the building. Of course the trees had changed. Some were gone, others had grown. The lines of the vineyard had also evolved somewhat, and now the surrounding area bristled with buildings and electric poles. Modern housing encumbered the horizon, but the perspectives fit perfectly, only slightly transposed and compacted by the artist. More than a century earlier, a local painter had set himself up with his easel in this very spot, prepared his paints, drawn his sketches, and placed his spots of color amid a group of grape harvesters.

All he had to do was turn his head a little to the right, toward the south, and Dr. Baldès's overmantel appeared in turn, with the emblematic facade of the Château Haut-Brion, its two conical turrets transported to the wing as if to lighten the main central square of the building. The earth was combed as straight as a die, and not a single rebellious plant intruded. Benjamin paused for a moment. He already knew what he would discover but waited a few seconds to better enjoy the instant when he would find the landscape of the third painting.

A quarter turn to the right, toward the west, and he saw it by just looking at the bottom of the hill. The Moniales Haut-Brion was there, yes, hidden behind the plants, but very much there. It was so obvious. He would have realized it earlier, had he taken the time to think about it. Benjamin kicked himself for not being more perceptive, and he silently thanked Ferdinand Ténotier. The third painting was right there under his nose, and, unlike the other two, it had to be the only one that didn't correspond exactly with reality. The Moniales château was now obscured by greenery the landscaper Michel Bonfin had planted at the beginning of the nineteenth century. The painter had enjoyed a clear view, as the trees were less filled in and shorter, and he had been able to make out the flow of the Peugue, the moss-covered stone fountain, the small pink marble chapel, and the grapevines. With a little imagination, it was easy to picture the scene.

Virgile was standing off to the side, but he quickly picked up on his employer's speculation. He walked up and squinted, examining the landscape and forming a frame between the right angles of his thumbs and index fingers.

"In my opinion, sir, if you pretend the strip housing, apartment buildings, and suburban homes around the estate are not there, you can almost believe that…"

Benjamin imitated him, closing one eye to focus.

"Indeed, all that's missing are the grape harvesters," he said, as he was sure that the third painting had workers in the vineyards, like the others.

"So there you have it, your third overmantel. It's the Moniales."

"Unfortunately, that is not so. Reality is just an illusion, my dear Virgile. Only the artist's eye captures the truth, even if it seems distorted or interpreted. Do you see what I mean? I would really like to know where that piece of truth is hiding."

"We're not really going to hit up all the antique dealers in the region, are we?" the assistant asked with a little too much familiarity.

"Watch what you say. I'm perfectly capable of doing that," Benjamin replied. There was no joking in his tone.

Virgile rubbed his neck and felt it best to keep a certain distance. He regretted overstepping his bounds and saying something that could have been interpreted as a lack of respect.

"There is something bothering me, sir. What's the link between the Moniales and the Haut-Brion estate?"

"There isn't one today, except that they share the same *terroir* on the Graves plateau. The Moniales estate belongs to the Fonsegrive-Massepain family, and it has since the beginning of the nineteenth century, when it was purchased by Aristide Fonsegrive, a wine trader in Bordeaux and a direct ancestor of Denis's wife, Thérèse. During the French Revolution, when all the land belonging to the Church was confiscated, the estate became state property."

"It once belonged to the Church?"

"To the Order of Our Lady of the Moniales, for two centuries. At first, there was nothing but a small watermill surrounded by prairie and vineyards. Toward the end of his life, Jean de Pontac, who was the true founder of the Château Haut-Brion, thought he could gain a foothold in heaven by giving this parcel to a religious order. He was a bourgeois Bordeaux merchant and had bought the manorial rights. He was born in 1488 and died in 1589, was married three times, and had fifteen children. He was a busy one."

"He lived to be one hundred and one?" asked Virgile.

"Don't you count fast. Jean de Pontac did, in fact, live under the reigns of kings Louis XII, François I, Henri II, Charles IX, and Henri III. Some years are good and age exceptionally well," Benjamin sighed. "I have tasted some wines that have crossed the century and lived through a dozen French presidents."

The winemaker sat down on a small pile of stones at the foot of the water tower and invited his assistant to do the same. He then recited the full details of the Pontac family dynasty. Arnaud II, the fourth son of the centenary, was the bishop of Bazas, and his funeral procession was over nine miles long. Geoffroy, president of the Bordeaux parliament, lived in the Daurade, a private mansion overflowing in gold and mirrors. Arnaud III wallowed in the same luxury as his father and became the first president of the local parliament. And finally there was François-Auguste, who also headed up the Bordeaux parliament and was the last direct Pontac descendent to own Haut-Brion.

"From then on, things became terribly complicated," the winemaker continued. "François-Auguste lived in such luxury, the château was seized twice to pay his debts. When his sister, Marie-Thérèse, inherited the estate in 1694, the land was split up, and she managed to keep only two thirds of it. I'll spare you the details of who slept with whom and who was the widow of whom."

"Too bad! That's often the most interesting information!" said Virgile.

"You'd be disappointed. There is nothing very spicy, just stories of alliances and marriages for money. No small favors or pillow talk, I fear. At this stage, François Delphin d'Aulède de Lestonnac, Marie-Thérèse's son—she had married the owner of Château Margaux—inherited both Haut-Brion and Margaux. And that explains a rather astonishing tradition. Haut-Brion, which is in the Graves, is still classified as a Médoc premier cru, in accordance with a very ancient formulation that did not take into account its geography, but rather its age-old noble codes of usage."

"And that's still the case today?"

"Don't forget that Bordeaux is a land of traditions. Never forget that! So, stop me if it gets too complicated, okay, Virgile? This François Delphin, marquis of Margaux and owner of Haut-Brion, died in 1746 and passed down his land to his sister, Catherine d'Aulède de Lestonnac, the widow of Count François-Joseph de Fumel, who had a son named Louis, who would die at a very young age. Are you still with me?"

"Yes, yes. I'm closing my eyes to concentrate better."

"In the end, it was the grandson, Joseph de Fumel, who developed the estate, adding an orangery, operational buildings, and very large grounds. He also contributed greatly to the renown of Haut-Brion wine abroad, trading with England and Sweden. He was guillotined in 1794. From then on, the same lot was reserved for the Moniales. The estate was sold as state property, and Charles-Maurice Talleyrand bought it in 1801. At the time, he was Napoleon's minister of foreign affairs, as you know."

"Is he the one who limped? The one Napoleon called 'shit in silk stockings'?" Virgil asked, knitting his eyebrows.

"The description is terse but rather well summarized. Tallyrand was a grim man but brilliant. He is said to have given this advice about Haut-Brion, and it's guidance that people should heed more often. 'Before raising such a nectar to one's lips, hold the glass high, and look at it, sniff it at length, and then, set your glass down, and talk about it!' Very perceptive, isn't it?"

"Well put," Virgile said, nodding.

"Tallyrand did not stay at Haut-Brion for long. He sold everything in 1804. He had other things to do, and he didn't have a farmer's soul. You have to be a little bit of a farmer to love a land like this one, even if your coffers are full of gold, and you're chock full of honors. As was the Larrieu family, which was next in line. They were a dynasty of jurists with a number of more or less happy successors throughout the nineteenth century. After Joseph-Eugène Larrieu and his son, Amédée, came Eugène, who inherited in 1873 and went on to impose a near-military discipline on his winemakers. This was an important step, as the Larrieu family bought the third that belonged to the countess of Vergennes and united the domaine again. They always had energetic stewards, and you have to admit that were it not for Eugène Larrieu's authoritarian determination, the estate would have suffered more from the Phylloxera and mildew epidemics that ravaged all of Bordeaux's vineyards. He managed the estate with an iron fist until 1896, but he had no heir. His vines were prolific, but he was dry."

The ups and downs of Haut-Brion's history had loosened Benjamin's tongue, and he was in brilliant form. He enjoyed initiating Virgile into this world, with its codes that were sometimes difficult to decrypt. He went on to talk about the various problems linked to the joint ownership of the property and the Compagnie Algérienne, a bank that owned the château for a time before selling it to the extravagant André Gibert. He was a stickler for rules but loved experimenting. He also lacked an heir, so the estate ended up in the hands of the American financier Clarence Dillon after several months of harsh negotiations. On May 13, 1935, the Château Haut-Brion was transferred to the Dillon family. Over time, the majority of its heirs were attached enough to the estate to forget the bustle of New York and show an interest in its operations. Some even settled there.

"Okay, I'll stop there! I think I've overwhelmed you," Benjamin said, getting up.

They returned to Bordeaux at dusk. Benjamin dropped his assistant off at the Place de la Victoire and drove down the Cours de la Marne to reach the Saint-Jean train station. He double-parked and ran to the departure hall to get some pictures made in a photo booth. The harsh flash surprised him as he tried to put on an impassive, dignified expression. The result was astonishing, to say the least. The four small pictures showed just three-quarters of his face. One eye was half closed, the other was red from the flash, and he had a splotch of white light running across his forehead. Benjamin was quite amused by his startled look. "Clearly, reality is nothing but an illusion," he thought, slipping the photos into his inside jacket pocket. He was sure that Pascale Dartigeas would be talented enough to rework his portrait and reproduce his features accurately.

The end-of-April evening breeze was warm. As he left the train station, he removed a parking ticket from under the windshield wiper of his Mercedes and tossed it onto the back seat. Benjamin Cooker had just spent an excellent day.

9

Do you think you can suffocate on your own vomit?" Virgile asked, folding the newspaper.

"Spare me the details, please," the winemaker said, looking disgusted.

The winemaker hadn't read more than the first paragraph of the article in the latest edition of the *Sud-Ouest* before setting it on the edge of the table.

It was late morning, still chilly, and there were only a few scattered patrons at the Régent's outside tables. A handful of regulars, comfortably sheltered by a large red awning and ensconced in their rattan chairs, were taking in the city's moods. Some were deep in their newspapers, not paying any attention to their neighbors, while others were sipping their coffee in seats at the front to better observe the comings and goings on the Place Gambetta, with its buses swerving along the Cours Clemenceau and young women hurrying between stopped cars.

Virgile had joined Benjamin a little late. He sputtered an excuse and immediately started talking about the story in the paper. The headline read, "Pessac loses its living archives." The story took up two columns but didn't have any pictures.

The quiet Cité Frugès, a modern architectural jewel designed by Le Corbusier, is in mourning. Mr. Ferdinand Ténotier, a professor of medieval history at the University of Bordeaux for thirty years, was found dead yesterday morning in his apartment. The postman, who was delivering his pension payment, discovered the old man slumped on his kitchen table, his face lying in the remains of a meal he had regurgitated. This solitary, sometimes extravagant man, once married to an aristocrat from Andalusia, was a leading expert in Pessac history. Mr. Ténotier studied at the École des Chartes and had a comparative literature degree from La Sorbonne. He spoke Latin, Greek, Hebrew, Armenian, and several other languages. In addition, he received many honors for his 1954 annotated translation of Don Quixote from sixteenth-century Spanish. He was also the author of a popular pamphlet on the history of Pessac, which, unfortunately, is out of print. No stone in the town was a secret to him, and his tragic death at the age of seventy eight is a great loss for our region.

"It's strange. The funeral arrangements aren't mentioned in the article," Virgile said.

"I'm not surprised."

"They're not going to bury him like a dog, are they?"

"You never know. I suppose they'll do an autopsy to make sure his death was accidental," Benjamin said, getting up from the table.

"You think so?"

"What I think is that it is high time we get to Moniales and check some things out. Don't you agree, Virgile?"

"If you say so."

§ § §

Alexandrine de la Palussière was already at work when they arrived at the cellars. She had checked the steel tanks, taking a few new samples before intervening to treat the contamination. She was wearing beige leather espadrilles, plain linen pants, and a sky-blue cashmere sweater. She looked like someone fresh and ready for a golf resort or a sailing club for indulged teenagers. Her bob cut, held back by the never-changing mother-of-pearl hairband, brought out the best in her smooth face.

She carefully descended the stepladder she had been perched on to join her employer, who was fretting at the door of the building, his face pale. Alexandrine put on a smile as she walked over to him with a lightly swaying step. She shook the winemaker's hand and gave Virgile a look-over. She thought he might actually be nice, but his good looks were a little too impertinent. Denis Massepain had just arrived from his office, where a phone call had tied him up for an hour.

"Excuse me," he said, uncomfortable. "I didn't even have time to greet Mademoiselle de la Palussière. I was on the phone with some American buyers. Business must go on."

He said hello to the young woman, who accepted his apology immediately and introduced herself. The owner apologized again and thanked her for coming. She thanked him for his trust and said she was sorry, in turn, for not introducing herself earlier.

"Where are we, Alexandrine?" Benjamin asked, putting an end to the unproductive civilities.

"I considered two different approaches. I didn't have the time to discuss them with you, but I quickly abandoned the idea of using diethyl pyrocarbonate in its new dimethyl form. It is not stable enough, because it is too quick to hydrolyze into ethanol and carbonic gas. In my opinion, that could leave minor secondary products that might give the wine an overly fruity aroma. In addition, we would have to use over two hundred milligrams per liter to totally destroy the infection."

"That's unthinkable!" Benjamin said. "It is absolutely impossible, and it's forbidden by European regulations."

"In that case, I think that we should fall back on the more traditional sulfur dioxide treatment. It's the only alternative."

Denis Massepain listened attentively. He had been trained as an embryologist and had spent years working in the pharmaceutical industry, so he understood what the alchemist was saying. Virgile, however, found it too esoteric for his taste.

Alexandrine continued her presentation as if she were addressing only her employer. "Cleaning the barrels was crucial. Now the wood should be healthy, which will prevent any yeast proliferation in the cellars. We are doing a residual analysis of the cleaned barrels, but if the work was done properly, there should be no problem."

Virgile did not falter.

"I have no doubt about the results," Benjamin said dryly.

"I hope not," Alexandrine responded. "All we have left to do then is to add the sodium dioxide, and I think that will be done in an hour or two. I used the most recent readings to determine the pH of each lot to adjust the dosage. I won't use wicks, because they are not precise enough."

The biologist was referring to a technique dating from the eighteenth century that was still in use. Sulfur candles, introduced by the Dutch, were nothing more than wicks dipped in sulfur that produced a sanitizing gas when burned in wine barrels. The winemaker had often used them to eliminate germs and minimize their effect. He knew the advantages and limitations of this system, which had been used to save some great wines while preserving their purity and aromatic characteristics.

"What method do you suggest?" he asked.

"I will use effervescent sulfur that allows for more precise dosing. It is easier, although the trouble with metabisulfite discs is homogenous distribution of the sodium dioxide. We'll have to stir from time to time. Mr. Massepain can make sure the lees get in suspension on a daily basis."

"Virgile will stop by and do it, don't worry," Benjamin said. "He will also take samples from the tanks and bring them to the lab so you can monitor the treatment."

"As you wish," Alexandrine answered without looking at the assistant.

Benjamin wished his biologist luck and then motioned to Denis and Virgile to follow him.

"That woman is a gem," he said softly. "But honestly, I prefer sparing you another presentation on yeast dosing, active ingredients, gauging antiseptics, and all those damned molecules. They are enough to make you hate wine."

The Moniales estate owner would have chuckled, were the situation not so serious, and Virgile held back a quiet laugh himself for fear of appearing mean-spirited. "Denis, I'm going to talk to you as a friend and certainly not as a client," the winemaker said suddenly. "In any case, you're not a client, and you never will be. Don't even expect to get a bill!"

"But I insist!" Massepain said firmly.

"We can talk about that later. We have another matter to discuss. I would like you to tell me very frankly if you have had any trouble with a member of your staff."

"No, not at all. I even gave some raises not so long ago. Overall, my employees are not complaining, and I must say that I have been very touched by their reaction to this problem."

"Are you absolutely sure there hasn't been any problem?"

"No, I told you. You have seen their attitude. Everyone is working late and not counting their hours."

"Who is responsible for the cellar keys and the security system?"

"Why are you asking me all these question?" Massepain asked.

"Answer me. Who has the keys? Who knows the code to the alarm?"

"Two of us: the steward and I."

"Nobody else? Not even your secretary?"

"No. And I don't even want to hear what you are trying to insinuate. Jean Laborde has been my steward for years. He's a wonderful man and has my total trust. It sounds like you…"

"I have to, Denis," interrupted Benjamin. "We are more and more convinced that this infection did not get here on its own. I don't want to make any accusations, but it could be an act of treachery. Virgile agrees with me, isn't that so?"

The assistant nodded.

"But you've seen infections like this in other cellars, haven't you?" Denis Massepain asked. "This is something that happens to others. It was my turn."

"This is true," acquiesced the winemaker. "And I won't disclose the names of the estates where I've had to intervene. But each time, it was the result of negligence or questionable sanitation. That is totally impossible here."

"What do you plan to do then?"

"Have there been any recent visitors who have had access to the cellars? Reporters? Salespeople? Interns? You get the picture, any outsiders coming and going?"

"There was a magazine reporter this winter, with a photographer. They interviewed me for an article, but we only went through the cellars to take some pictures. That's all."

"Have there been any other visitors?"

"Very few, and they stayed mainly in the tasting room. I don't like to have people in the barrel room. Most of the time it is locked, as you know."

"Have there been any interns from the wine school? You must get some in from time to time."

"I've had four since last year, each for a month and no longer. You know that if you really want to train young people, you need to take time, and I don't have a lot of it to spare. We don't have enough staff."

"What became of these interns? Have you seen them since?"

"I haven't had any contact with them. Some must have graduated, and others are probably still at school."

"Could you give me their names, along with the names of all your usual staff and their addresses?"

"My secretary will have all that information. Follow me."

They went to the reception area near the entrance gate. They climbed the stairs, consulted a large green notebook, and made several photocopies that Benjamin gave to Virgile.

When they got back to the Mercedes, they heard thunder. In the distance, the skies over the ocean were rumbling, and a west wind was carrying in dark, threatening clouds. A few heavy drops of cold rain came down on the two men, who hurried to put the convertible top up. The assistant held the handful of photocopies over his head to protect himself. Benjamin grabbed them out of his hands and shielded them under his jacket. The pavement gave off the sweet aroma of wet dust.

"Hurry, Virgile! Get this car covered up. This is good weather for winemakers. Here you could say 'April showers, good for wine and flowers.' "

10

Grangebelle glistened behind the flowing shapes of the poplar trees. Elisabeth had lit tens of small candles and placed them along the windowsills at the front of the house. Benjamin parked his convertible near the wine cellar, checked the date on his watch, and suddenly realized that he had turned fifty at exactly 12:15 that afternoon. He had crossed that critical threshold of a half a century, which he had long worried about. Bacchus celebrated his arrival as he did every other evening. He jumped up and put his muddy paws on his master's light blue shirt. Benjamin brushed him off and hurried to the house. His wife was waiting for him in the hallway with an amused smile. He hugged her and whispered in her ear, "I can't believe it. The big five-zero, can you imagine?"

"Happy birthday, my Benjamin. I can't wait to open that 1953 Gruaud-Larose that you've been hiding away all these years."

"We're going to enjoy that one," Benjamin said, sniffing the aromas coming out of the kitchen. "It smells like the seaside, like we're on vacation, my love."

"I prepared you an Arcachon stew. The sea scallops were superb. And I invited the Delfrancs."

"That's an excellent idea. I haven't seen them in ages. I'll bring up a few bottles of white too. We'll start with the Gruaud-Larose."

He went down into his sanctuary, a small, well-ordered cellar, meticulously—almost compulsively—arranged, where he kept his best stock, the rare vintages, bottles from prestigious estates and exceptional wines few people ever got to taste. Alain and Chantal Delfranc were among the privileged few who could appreciate such an honor. The couple had recently moved to Saint-Estèphe and opened a bed and breakfast whose reputation had quickly spread across the Médoc. Alain had worked for years in the French intelligence service. He had taken an early retirement so that Chantal and he could leave Paris and launch the venture they had dreamed about for years. The two men had met in the 1970s, during the carefree days when Alain was still a police intern, and Benjamin was tending the bar at the Caveau de la Huchette. They had remained in touch, and when Alain's project took shape, the winemaker helped the couple find an old manor house that they transformed into an upscale guesthouse before opening one of the best restaurants in the area.

Alain was a refined epicurean and an inventive cook who grew unjustly forgotten heirloom vegetables and loved promising small-estate wines. In his new role as guesthouse owner and restaurateur, he spent much of his time in the cozy warmth of his kitchen, convinced that a passion was not fully experienced until it was shared. Chantal followed along, bringing with her a perpetual good mood. She decorated the premises with a clear taste for simple furniture, worn leather, and metallic accessories, balancing beige and chocolate brown to produce a rare, authentic feel and old-world charm. Chantal was graceful, despite her plump waistline, sassy nose, and mischievous eyes. She lived life with a candid sensuality that threw some people off—those who couldn't see beyond appearances. What could be construed as easy virtue was simply a genuine, open interest in all the pleasures that came her way.

Benjamin grabbed two bottles of a dry white Château Haut-Brion. It was criminal to open this 1989 now, but to hell with expert recommendations! Life was too short, and he would not wait another fifty years before tasting it. When he came back up from the sanctuary, the Delfrancs had just arrived. Bacchus was barking. Elisabeth was untying her apron, and Chantal was already joking about Benjamin's respectable age. Alain smiled as he set his raincoat down on one of the chairs in the entrance.

The bottles of white wine went into a bucket of ice, and everyone sat around a coffee table in the living room to taste the illustrious 1953 Gruaud-Larose that the winemaker had decanted much too late. This evening, every sacrilege was permitted. Benjamin slowly unwrapped the gift the Delfrancs offered him. He was intrigued by the medium-sized flat box, undid the ribbon, and was careful not to tear the wrapping paper. He slowly opened the cardboard and discovered a bright ink drawing dating from 1933.

"You're out of your mind! You shouldn't have!"

"Of course I had too!" Alain said. "I'm no crazier than you are opening that Gruaud-Larose as old as your arteries."

"You're mad," Benjamin said again, holding the sketch along its edges. "I can't believe it. An original from the Nicolas catalog illustrated by Jean Hugo. You can't find these anywhere."

"That's proof you're wrong," Chantal said, lifting the glass to her lips. "You know that Alain can find anything, anywhere, whenever, and, well, however!"

Benjamin seemed almost uncomfortable and did not know how to thank his friends. He took a sip of wine, with the full tasting ritual, because he had to find a way to calm his emotions. Elisabeth disappeared and returned with a steaming tureen.

"Let's eat. It's hot. I made a stew, so there are no starters."

"I've been waiting to taste this famous stew of yours!" Alain said, rubbing his hands.

He immediately asked for the recipe. Elisabeth didn't hold out on him and told him every detail: the puree of carrots, leeks, tomatoes, onions, and shallots that she cooked over low heat for twenty minutes before she strained it through a fine sieve; the salt, pepper, and saffron dosed with care, along with the hint of cayenne pepper; the mussels cooked in a white Graves; the juice strained before the addition of the delicate langoustine tails; the sea scallops sautéed in hot butter; and the crème fraîche used to thicken the sauce, which was then reduced for at least three minutes.

Everyone got a generous serving, and there was a moment of silence before the compliments started flying. As usual, Elisabeth accepted her triumph with modesty and raised her glass of white Haut-Brion. They toasted Benjamin and then talked about all manner of things, about time flying by too quickly, about children living too far away, about vacation memories, bottling in Bordeaux, about wine, as always, and about gastronomy too, about old English cars, unreadable books and boring movies, about all those little essential and useless things that strengthened the bonds among the four friends a little more each time they met. They ignored politics, however, not because they weren't interested, but mostly because they didn't want to chance miry paths where friendships could get stuck. Spiritual concerns were also only mentioned in passing, with just a few allusions tainted with irony. Benjamin knew his friend was resolutely atheist, and he himself believed that one could not reasonably talk about God with a flute of Champagne in his hand.

Dessert was sumptuous, without any candles or ritual song. Benjamin hated those childish manifestations. Elisabeth knew him too well to commit that faux pas, which would have ruined their enjoyment of the Bavarian cream presented on a caramelized sheet of puff pastry and covered with roasted chopped pistachios. They drank coffee in the living room, and no one wanted an after-dinner spirit. Alain lit a pipe of Amsterdamer, and Benjamin dug around in his little rosewood box to find a Lusitania from Partagas, which he then lit with relish. The women stayed at a distance, complaining about the smoke that kept them from enjoying the perfume samples they extracted from their handbags. Benjamin took advantage of the moment to remove a piece of paper from his jacket pocket. He unfolded it and held it out to his friend.

"Do you still have any contact with your former colleagues in intelligence?"

"With some, yes. I've got a friend from Paris who was transferred to Gironde. We see each other from time to time."

"Could you get me some information about these people?"

"What kind of information?"

The winemaker briefly summarized what had happened to Denis Massepain, and without going into the details, he shared his suspicions. He didn't want to incriminate the employees on the list; he just wanted to make sure there was no doubt about their integrity. He insisted that any inquiries be made with complete discretion in a totally unofficial way.

"I'll call you tomorrow," Alain said. "Don't tell me anything else, or I'll end up becoming interested."

§ § §

The following day dragged out. It was both lethargic and feverish. Benjamin waited for Alain's phone call and couldn't concentrate on his writing. He had gotten up rather late and had drunk his tea mechanically, nibbling on a few broken pieces of Melba toast. Finally, he holed up in his office to outline the nth draft of his text about the citadel.

"The rocks of Blaye have seen many battles. This city, perched on a steep cliff one hundred and twenty feet above the Gironde Estuary, has been the object of everyone's desire. Since the time of the Gauls and the Romans, the Visigoths, the Vikings, and the Plantagenets, there have been bloody battles, distant echoes of which…"

"Elisabeth," Benjamin shouted down to the living room, "Don't stay on the phone long. I'm waiting for a call."

He walked out to the deck that overlooked vineyards and played with Bacchus for quite a while, showing a clear lack of enthusiasm as he threw and threw again an iridescent blue plastic bone that Margaux had brought from the United States the previous summer. Then he tossed the hideous object into the garbage can as his dog looked on in disbelief.

Elisabeth offered him a light meal, which he refused. He chose to close himself up again in his office, where he reread some juicy passages of *Le Chic Anglais*, James Darwen's precious guide for the perfect gentleman. The author's sharp witticisms, peremptory precepts, and delicious bad faith failed to make Benjamin laugh. He set the work down with exaggerated nonchalance in an attempt to control his nervousness. Then he tried to force himself to relax. After five minutes spent drifting, his feet up on his leather Empire desk, he decided to waste away the afternoon of waiting by focusing on the upkeep of his footwear. A John Lobb lover, no matter how wealthy he was or how many people he employed, could never entrust his shoe polishing to anyone else. What could be more personal than shining his black leather Oxfords and buffing his brown loafers? He had selected each pair with great care on trips to Paris, and he never missed an opportunity to visit the shop on the Boulevard Saint-Germain to explore new collections and find old classics. He preferred, however, the store on St. James Street, which he visited every time he went to see his parents in London.

Benjamin spent more than three hours polishing his Lobbs, tirelessly massaging the leather with a light concentric movement that accentuated the shine. He took pleasure in observing the fullness of the grain, the hue, and the amber transparency of his shoes, a harmony just as subtle as the one experienced by his eye, nose, and mouth when he tasted a grand cru wine. The winemaker was almost calm when the telephone finally rang.

"I handled your list," Alain said. "My former colleagues still remember me, and they took care of it in a day. Maybe you could send them a case of Médoc."

"I'm listening."

"I don't have much to say about the staff members. The steward got a speeding ticket, and one of the workers has filed for divorce, but other than that, there is nothing on record. They all lead rather calm lives."

"And the four interns?"

"No problem there, either. None have records. They work hard and don't make any waves. Edouard Camps is still in school and is preparing his dissertation. Antoine Armel found a job on an estate in the Touraine, where he is assistant cellar master. Sébastien Guéret took over the family's printing business after his father had a car accident, and David Morin works in sales for a Cognac merchant."

"So there's nothing that stands out, then?" Benjamin said, disappointed.

"Sorry, bad luck."

Benjamin hung up after promising to stop by the Delfrancs place to taste his sweetbreads cooked in a Bordeaux sparkling wine. Then he tried to rewrite the piece on the Blaye fortress, although he knew the end result would not be the best.

"Some say that the body of Roland de Roncevaux lies under Blaye. Charlemagne's troops transported his corpse in a gold coffin on the back of two mules to the Saint-Romain de Blaye basilica, which was buried in the seventeenth century by Vauban's landfilling work. Were you to dig, you would perhaps find

Durandal's sword and the valiant knight's ivory horn that was immortalized by the song…"

Benjamin threw the paper into the trash and finally joined his wife, apologizing for being so disagreeable.

11

Benjamin and Elisabeth could barely hear the bustling Place Saint-Michel on the other side of heavy church doors. They were kneeling near the central aisle, observing the sanctimonious in Sunday dress desert the benches. The Mass had been mediocre. The sermon had lacked verve, and members of the flock had either dozed or been distracted. The Cooker couple waited until the organist's last notes fell silent. Then they walked out into the square in front of the church. A flea market had invaded the space at dawn. A colorful crowd moved around the dozens of improvised stands. A huge variety of objects was laid out on the ground: coffee grinders without handles, scratched vinyl records, Louis-Philippe armoires that had been too well restored, stolen car radios, garden ironworks, dusty engravings, windproof lighters, and military medals. Benjamin nosed about but didn't find anything that caught his eye, with the exception of a corkscrew with a brass handle shaped like a pair of legs, one of them with a garter belt. He paid next to nothing for it. Elisabeth followed him, looking detached, and then stopped in front of an Art Deco sugar bowl that she bought without bothering to haggle.

"I need to stop in to see the art restorer," the winemaker said. "Her workshop is open on Sunday mornings."

"Let's be quick about it, Benjamin. I'd like to get home."

Pascale Dartigeas greeted the couple with a smile that lit up her face and highlighted her blue-gray eyes. She was standing in front of a seascape whose colors were in dire need of cleaning.

"Mr. and Mrs. Cooker! To what do I owe the pleasure?"

"You asked me for a picture to redo that cellar master's portrait on the Toussaint Roussy."

"Indeed, show me."

The winemaker held out the photo-booth pictures and waited for Pascale Dartigeas's reaction.

"I don't mean to be rude, Mr. Cooker, but you look horrible in these pictures. Don't you agree, Mrs. Cooker?"

"I haven't even seen these. Show me," she said. "Yuck, it would have been hard to make you any uglier."

"What can I do with a face like that?" Pascale said, a little vexed.

"I'm counting on your talent to tidy it up," Benjamin said with a laugh. "You speak the truth, so paint me with the same honesty."

"I'll work from memory," she said, looking him straight in the eye, as if she wanted to grab her client's mischievous expression and natural distinction.

Elisabeth had wandered to the back of the workshop and was examining the soft pink flesh of a Baroque angel that was flying in the swirls of a long purple scarf.

"Have you made any progress on the overmantel?" Benjamin asked. "I don't see your intern."

"Julie is not here today, but she is working on it. Don't worry," the restorer said. "It will be finished at the end of the month. Your overmantel is intriguing. I just talked to a man who was examining it and said he owns one just like it."

"Say again?"

"A rather corpulent man in a wheelchair who came in not more than ten minutes ago."

"Do you know who he is?" Benjamin asked, suddenly nervous.

"Not at all. It was the first time I'd seen him. He just told me that his was in better shape and that all he had done was clean it by rubbing a cut potato on the varnish. A heresy! That's an old wives tale that never worked and could ruin a canvas."

"When did he leave?" Benjamin asked.

"I told you. Ten minutes ago. He went toward the bell tower. His wife was pushing the wheelchair. They can't be too far."

The winemaker quickly said good-bye, promising to come back during the week. He grabbed Elisabeth by the wrist, tearing her away from the flying angel. "Quick. It's important," he whispered into her ear. She barely had time to say good-bye to Pascale Dartigeas before she found herself outside the store, gripping her husband's arm. They walked quickly through the stands along the sidewalk in front of the Passage Saint-Michel, stepping over piles of old mechanical parts spread on the pavement, bumping into a grandfather clock, and nearly knocking over a very kitsch psychedelic lamp.

"What's happening, Benjamin?" Elisabeth asked, out of breath.

"We're looking for a man in a wheelchair."

"And you think we'll find him at the flea market?" she asked.

This was not her husband's first flight of fancy, and she was used to even more comical situations, but she felt completely lost. Benjamin summed up the conversation she had missed while she was contemplating the celestial creature.

"We absolutely have to find this fellow," Benjamin continued, using his hand to shield his eyes from the sun.

His wife did the same and slowly turned to examine the surroundings in a broad circular movement.

"Over there, to the right. That looks like a paraplegic," she said calmly.

"Where?"

"Near the café, on the other side of the square. His wife is helping him get in the car."

"I don't see anything!"

"To the right, I said. She is folding up the wheelchair and putting it in the trunk. It's a white station wagon with an antenna on the roof."

"I see it. By the time we cross the square, they'll be gone already. Follow me."

The couple ran to the convertible, which was parked on the Rue des Allamandiers. Benjamin started it with a six-cylinder roar that scared a crowd of bystanders, who stepped aside like a single person. Elisabeth held onto her seat as they sped around the church and came out on the Rue des Faures. The station wagon was already on the street that led to the Capucins market. Benjamin slowed down a little, reassured that he would not lose the car now. They drove up the Cours de l'Yser, after running a red light, and cut across the Cours de la Marne. When they arrived at the Place Nansouty, the white station wagon had already disappeared behind the clump of flowers in the center of the roundabout, having turned onto the street leading to the Saint-Jean train station.

"What the…?" Benjamin spit out, stopping behind a delivery van that was blocking the road.

"They turned left. Calm down," his wife said, putting a hand on his arm.

Benjamin impatiently drummed the steering wheel with his fingers as he waited for the van driver to deign to start up again. Then he rushed onto the Rue Pelleport and slowed down to look into the side streets.

"There they are," Elisabeth cried out. "They parked on the Rue de Cérons. On the left. She is unfolding the chair."

"It's one way. I'll have to take the next street and go around the block."

It took them only two minutes to drive around the block, but they arrived too late. They barely caught a glimpse of the wheelchair as it disappeared into a dull-looking building, and the entrance door clacked shut. Benjamin stopped his convertible in the middle of the street without turning on his blinker or turning off the engine. He walked up to 36 Rue de Cérons and read the enameled sign above the doorbell: "Yvonne Soulagnet. No soliciting."

"It's not right to disturb people this early on a Sunday afternoon. I'll come back tomorrow," he said to his wife. "Since we're in the neighborhood, let's go buy some *cannelés* from Laurent Lachenal's bakery, and we can pick up some of his sesame bread. I'm starving after this little adventure."

Benjamin felt a little muddled after spending two hours in traffic jams. He had just driven across greater Bordeaux without putting the top of the convertible up, breathing in gas fumes and collecting a layer of dust from the ongoing construction the entire way. When he finally turned onto the Rue de Cérons, he had no trouble finding a parking spot in front of number 36. He rang the bell several times before an elderly woman stuck her nose through a crack in the door, which was held firmly in place by a safety chain. He introduced himself, using a fake name. He didn't bother to provide any lengthy explanations, preferring to get directly to the point.

"I'm looking for a disabled man who was here yesterday. I know that he likes paintings, and I would like to talk to him about a canvas that could interest him."

"I live alone," the woman mumbled.

She had a husky voice that didn't seem to go with her frail body. Her wrinkled yellow complexion resembled a baked apple, and she had sparse hair and hunched shoulders.

"Excuse me for insisting, Mrs. Soulagnet, but I am sure that he will be happy to meet me. I have a painting that I'm certain will interest him."

"Another lousy painting that serves no purpose," the old woman said. "The house is full of them."

"I promise you that Mr. Soulagnet will really…"

"That's not his name! He's my son-in-law. Unfortunately. My poor daughter fell in love with a good-for-nothing, instead of his brother, who knew how to make money. It's a good thing my grandson was able to take over the business. Paintings don't feed the family!"

"You are right, Madame, but please, allow me to insist."

"You are stubborn, aren't you," the old woman chuckled.

"At least give me his name and address so that I can get in touch with him. I won't bother you anymore."

"Gilles Guéret. He is a printer in Bègles. You'll find him in the phone book. The *Béglais Pratique* free sheet is his. My grandson's Sébastien Guéret. He's in charge there now."

Then she let out a grumble in the guise of a good-bye and slammed the door.

Pensive, Benjamin slowly walked back to his Mercedes. He turned the key, began to leave the parking space, and then cut the engine. He grabbed his cell phone and called Virgile.

"Where are you?"

"Hello. I'm at Moniales. I'm finishing up with the samples to take them to the lab."

"We can see to that later."

"But, sir, Alexandrine is waiting for them."

"I said later! Does the name Sébastien Guéret ring a bell?"

There was a brief silence.

"He was an intern on the list. We went to the same wine school, but I didn't know him very well. He wasn't in my class. He is two years younger than I am. We talked to each other occasionally."

"Excellent. You will need to get in touch with him right away."

"How?"

"I don't know. Figure something out. He runs a printing business that publishes an advertising circular. Find something to sell, and go there now. It's in Bègles, the Guéret Press. It's not that complicated. I'm sure you'll find it in the industrial park."

"Something to sell?"

"Anything, it doesn't matter. Be there in a half an hour."

"Maybe my car? It's a rundown Renault 5. I don't have any idea how much it's worth."

"It doesn't matter, I told you. Run an ad and try to talk to this Sébastien Guéret. Dig around, ask questions, and bring back what you can."

"So I don't even go to the lab?" Virgile asked.

"It's urgent! You should be on your way already!"

"I'd say, sir, that things are picking up."

"It's about time!"

12

The printing firm's office was functional, with a clinical ugliness that reflected the tastes of the entrepreneurs who had located in the industrial park. Virgile approached the counter, looking somewhat timid, and grabbed an ad form. The secretary flashed a big smile.

"Madmoiselle, I'm not sure how to fill in this form."

"I'd be happy to help you."

"Well, I'd like to sell a, well, a somewhat old car. Actually, a really old car. Let's just say it's not in such good shape, and I don't exactly know how to describe it without scaring potential buyers away."

"That is a little difficult. You could say, 'Average condition. Passed inspection.' Or 'Sold as is. Price negotiable.' That's what people usually put, but I don't know anything about mechanics."

The conversation continued in a tone of flirtatious bantering. Virgile was playing for time, talking while he watched staff members come and go behind the window at the reception desk.

A surly and sad-looking secretary was yawning as she made photocopies. A man was pushing a cart of newspapers, and a worker in blue over-hauls was on his way to the employee restroom. After fifteen minutes, Benjamin's assistant had barely filled in ten lines of his ad form and was still chatting with the secretary, with no end to topics he cared nothing about. They talked about the Aquitaine Bridge project, the thirty-five-hour work week, the point-based driving license, the teachers strike, traffic jams at the Place de la Victoire, the next Johnny Hallyday concert, taxes, the bad season for the Girondins soccer team—so many things that reassured people about their ability to judge the state of the world.

He was beginning to feel desperate when he finally caught a glimpse of Sébastien Guéret's chubby cheeks. Their red hue betrayed poorly contained anger. The woman doing photocopies suffered a volley of reprimands and disappeared into the restroom, presumably to compose herself. Sébastien looked like a prosperous employer. An extra twenty pounds had been enough to settle him in life, giving him the self-satisfied look of a manager. When he approached the secretary, he took on an entirely different tone.

"Corinne, my dear, don't forget to bring in my signature book after lunch break," he said in a tender voice.

"Hey, we know each other, don't we?" Virgile said, sounding almost enthusiastic.

Sébastien Guéret looked up and saw him. Dimples appeared on his blotched chubby cheeks.

"That's right. You went to the wine school. Lanssien, isn't it? Mr. Virgile Lanssien!"

"We were not so formal back then."

"Sorry. It's a habit. What are you doing these days? Still in wine?"

"Oh, here and there. Some seasonal work on the estates when they need extra workers."

"I'm through with that. For a while, I thought I liked it, but after my father's accident, I had to take care of the business. And in the end, this is where I belong. If you've got some time, I can show you around. It's all brand new. We moved in last February. It was a lot of work but was worth it."

Sébastien wasn't exactly boastful, but he couldn't hide his pride. He invited Virgile to follow him and gave him a detailed description of each of the offices, starting with his, paneled in faux cherrywood veneer, followed by the accounting department, the invoicing computers, and the storage room. He went on about the growth in advertising revenues, thanks largely to the chamber of commerce and other institutions, paper he bought by the ton, rising prices, and storage issues. Virgile listened and nodded, pretending to be impressed. The personnel began to disappear for lunch.

"Don't forget to lock up after yourself!" Sébastien yelled out.

Then, lowering his voice without dropping the haughtiness, he added, "You have to keep a tight rein. Otherwise they'll be the end of you. Jerks! Believe me, it's not easy to run a business like this."

"I'm sure," Virgile said, giving him a knowing look.

"Some of them miss the old man and try to make things hard for me. I'll end up firing them one day or another, believe me. For that matter, I want to build an entirely new team."

"Times change," the winemaker's assistant said, thinking that might be an appropriate comment.

"If I had listened to my old man, we'd still be in the old neighborhood with run-down offices, only thirteen hundred square feet, crappy orders, and no potential for growth. His accident and his dead legs are really sad, but to be honest, he had turned down the wrong road awhile ago. No pun intended. He put all his money into printing catalogs for regional artists, for Sunday painters nobody knows about. His passion for lousy paintings cost us a lot of cash. Not to mention all those paintings he felt he had to buy to help out the freeloaders who didn't have enough cash to buy their own paint."

"He was like a patron."

"Patron, my ass! It almost ruined us, and my mother was happy when I finally took over the business. It's not always easy for her. She has to take him around in his wheelchair like a kid, wash him, and help him to the bathroom. You get the picture. But he leaves us alone now. We give him enough to buy one or two paintings from time to time, and that's all he asks. Come on, let me show you the best part yet."

He opened double doors that led to the machine room filled with shiny new rotary presses. Sébastien explained how each one worked, talked about the ten-year loan, the write-off, and how he had to keep changing the equipment for the graphic designers, particularly since *Le Béglais Pratique* had tripled its print run. Virgile was unable to stop him. Only the constant ringing of Sébastien's cell phone could get him to consent to a break.

"Excuse me. I'll be just a moment," Sébastien whispered. "If you want, you can wait for me in the hallway and have a coffee. I'll be right there."

"No problem. Take your time," Virgile said.

Once Virgile was alone, he walked around the deserted offices and looked under some piles of papers without really knowing what he was looking for or even if there was anything to find. He put a euro into the coffee machine and continued his tour with a burning-hot cup in hand. Sébastien Guéret's office was open. The lights were on, and his computer was snoozing. Virgile hit a key, and the screen lit up. He clicked on the "mail" file and scanned the list, which he judged to be of no interest, and then he opened the file called "projects." Several files were arranged under small colored icons. Virgile shuddered when he saw one called "Moniales" at the bottom of the list.

Without thinking, he clicked on the web browser icon and pulled up the Cooker&Co.com mail. It was taking forever. He logged in and sent the file to Cooker's address. His heart was pounding, and his shirt was suddenly damp. If only Sébastien could keep talking on the phone! The seconds dragged on. When the file was fully transferred, he opened the privacy settings window and erased any traces of what he had done.

He immediately returned to the lobby and had time to finish his coffee before Sébastien came back, excusing himself for being so long. Virgile told him he had an appointment in town and promised to stop by again. They said good-bye with an emphatic handshake.

As soon as he got into his rundown Renault 5, Virgile called his boss. "Sir? Are you at the lab? I'll be at the Allée de Tourny in fifteen minutes. Wait for me in your office. I just sent you an e-mail."

The Cooker & Co. inbox had several messages in it, including one from the owner of Vistaflores in the Argentine Pampas, where Benjamin was expected for the next winemaking season. There was also a note from Margaux, who wrote with news from New York, but Virgile immediately clicked on the Moniales file. It took awhile to download, but when he was finally able to open the document, Benjamin had a totally unfamiliar reaction.

"Holy shit! That can't be!"

The third overmantel was right there, lit up on the screen. Occupying the entire page was the Château Moniales Haut-Brion and its perfectly balanced facade, its rounded steps, its Doric columns, and its dark slate roof. The little chapel's tympanum was depicted in heavy brushstrokes. The painter had portrayed the building correctly, without respecting the enclosure's proportions. The vineyards appeared larger and spread beyond the walls. Because the overmantel had been photographed and scanned, the colors were exaggerated. The graphic designer who had laid out the accompanying information had been careful not to cover any part of the château's imposing structure, because it illustrated the significance of the announcement:

Moniales Residence
A corner of paradise two steps from central Bordeaux
Thirty upscale apartments just minutes from downtown
Near the university and shopping centers

Pool, tennis courts, playground, quality facilities
Treat yourself to country luxury in the heart of
the city!

"Well done, Virgile! Well done!"

They opened another file. This time it was a spreadsheet with construction costs, profitability thresholds, supplier estimates, and financial prospects that were a little difficult to decrypt. They scrolled through several dozen pages, a cold succession of measurements, percentages, and sums. Enough to make them dizzy.

Benjamin picked up his telephone and immediately called Alain Delfranc. At this hour, he had probably finished the lunch service and was quietly smoking his pipe at the window of the kitchen.

"I have news in the Moniales Haut-Brion case. We just discovered something huge."

"Where are you calling me from?"

"From my office on the Allée de Tourny. I'll admit that this is a little too big for me to handle all by myself."

"Okay, don't move," Alain ordered. "Starting now, don't touch anything else."

13

Taste that!"

Benjamin Cooker lifted the glass to eye level. Then he lowered it slowly, tilting it slightly in front of the white tablecloth to judge the wine's dark color and slightly oily texture as it slid slowly down the side.

"It's good," he said without showing any enthusiasm. "Very good, even. What is it?"

"Is the fabulous Cooker, the imperial winemaker, afraid of losing face?" Alain teased him gently.

"Not at all, my friend. I can tell you that there is sun in it. It's from the South. Perhaps it is made with syrah."

"You're getting warm. You're even quite close."

"Or rather, it's grenache noir and carignan. In any case, it is a blend like that. There is also some mourvèdre and perhaps a little cinsault."

"You're almost there."

"Its attack is not so subtle. It is well structured. You can feel the tannins. There are hints of berries and a slight touch of warm spices. It's well done."

"So?"

"Perhaps a Côte-du-Roussillon. You can smell the terraces, the stone, and the *tramontane* wind."

"You're burning hot."

"I'd say a wine from Collioure, with a characteristic personality and a very concentrated licorice finale. Perhaps it's Les Espérades from the Vial-Magnères domaine. It resembles that kind of wine."

"Damn. How do you do that?

"You do your job, and I do mine," the winemaker said, drinking another mouthful. "And what if you told me a little about yours."

"The one that used to be mine," Alain Delfranc corrected, lifting his index finger, "and that I was right to run away from, considering how rotten the world is!"

"Regardless, you did me a great service by taking the Moniales case to the police. Thanks to you, everything was handled quickly and efficiently."

"I think that if you had brought it to their attention yourself, they would have passed it from department to department," Alain admitted. "And they would have taken longer to order the search."

Benjamin poured himself another glass of Collioure and lit up a Villa Zamorano—a falsely rustic robusto from Honduras that he had heard about but had yet to taste. He settled into his armchair and let out a thick puff of gray smoke.

"So, now you can tell me exactly what he confessed to, our Guéret."

"Everything, absolutely everything! He didn't try to deny any of it. He was working for his uncle, Robert Guéret, who is, well, an unscrupulous real estate developer. The man helped his nephew when Gilles Guéret had his car accident. He invested in the printing presses and got bank loans to help Sébastien. In exchange, he asked for some small services. The kid wasn't a hard one to corrupt. He was a little snot who wanted to get ahead and, most of all, to prove to his mother that he could succeed where his father had failed."

"So it was Uncle Robert who planned the whole thing?" Benjamin asked, leaning back on the headrest.

"When Gilles Guéret had his accident, Sébastien's uncle got involved with the advertising circular. Sébastien was still an intern at the Moniales Haut-Brion, and the uncle wanted the kid to quit his oenology studies and take over the family business. Obviously, he put out some cash to persuade him. Before Sébastien left, however, the uncle saw his opportunity and asked his nephew for a favor. He had the kid make a wax imprint of the cellar keys. Apparently it is not very complicated. Sébastien took advantage of a moment of inattention on the steward's part to take the keys from his jacket, which was hanging near the door of the tank room, and he simply molded them in a special wax. Then he used the impressions to have the keys made. "

"So this wasn't something that Uncle Robert had spent a long time planning?" Benjamin said, setting down his empty glass.

"Not at all. One day when he was picking up his nephew at the château, it dawned on him that he could ruin Denis Massepain's life and offer to buy the estate at a rock-bottom price. Then he could build luxury apartments. No kidding. An estate of that standing, with several acres of trees and a small brook, has great appeal to developers. But that you saw on the documents."

"Yes, I saw. But that doesn't explain how they managed to get past the alarm."

"Guéret Jr. had overheard a conversation between Denis and the steward. One of them had mentioned a year, but it seemed out of context. Guéret realized that it was actually the code to the alarm. When he returned to put that damned yeast into the barrels, he entered the four numbers, and the alarm was turned off. He's not dumb! In fact, he's quite clever, because he specifically chose to pollute only some of the barrels so it wouldn't look like a malicious act."

"Absolutely. For the uncle and the nephew, it was just the first part of a strategy designed to drain Massepain's morale and put a proverbial knife to his throat. In any case, they intended to go as far as they needed to get their hands on the Moniales. They were ready to act as soon as their attacks succeeded. You saw how the uncle used Sébastien to build his marketing campaign for the luxury apartments even before the yeast had done its job. It was all in perfect order—starting with the overmantel used in the initial advertising. The whole campaign included posters, brochures, ads, and other promotional materials, all produced free of charge by the Guéret presses, of course!"

"And the overmantel…"

"That is another story. It is, for that matter, exclusively your story. Had you not gone out looking for that painting and then instinctively put two and two together when you discovered the connection to Sébastien, this crime would have played out. Nobody would have known. For that matter, I would like to know how many dirty deeds of the kind have been carried out in the Pessac and Talence areas! Behind all those buildings, luxury apartments, and suburban houses there must be some pretty sleazy politicking, scheming, bribing, intimidation, and power plays."

"Better not to imagine them. What good does it do? But how did they get their hands on that overmantel?"

"That was just by chance. Sébastien's father had bought the painting some time ago, and it had been lying around in a back hallway. The son had known about it since he was little, and he thought it would be good for the marketing campaign. Very chic! Even small-time swindlers can have class."

"Alain, I have to admit that I have been dishonest about something."

"It's time for the great confession!" the innkeeper said as he lit his pipe again.

"Yes, I must confess that I did something really ugly. It was a dirty trick you should never, ever pull on a friend."

Alain Delfranc started to turn pale.

"Are you serious, Benjamin? Or are you joking?"

"No, I'm serious. And if I tell you, promise me you won't tell anyone."

"Okay, okay."

"Your Collioure. I knew what it was with the first mouthful. I wrote about it last week for an English magazine."

"Cheater! And on top of that, you dragged out the pleasure, just so I'd wonder if there was a tiny chink in your winemaker's armor?"

"No, no. Just to make fun of myself."

§ § §

He made the decision when he woke up. He would use the first introduction to Blaye he had written. Just to be sure, Benjamin reread his new attempts to describe it and ended up throwing them away. He then called his editor to tell him there would be no modifications, with the exception of three words he absolutely had to change: "milksop" for "coward," "bloody" for "bloodthirsty," and "diverse," which fit better than "contrasted." When he hung up, he did not feel all that self-assured and was afraid that his final instructions would not be followed. He drank two cups of tea and decided to take Bacchus on a walk to clear his mind.

He didn't return until lunch, his boots caked with clay and his face damp with perspiration. The dog was in no better shape than his master. His tongue was hanging out. He was dragging his paws, and he didn't even bother to bark when Virgile's Renault 5 came speeding up Grangebelle's gravel drive.

"Hello, Mr. Cooker. Your friend Denis has sent over four cases of Moniales Haut-Brion to thank you for what you did."

"Of course you told him that tomorrow I'm off to Burgundy and that I would stop by to see him when I get back."

"I'll be sure to do so. When you are gone, I'll drop in to make sure everything is going well, but we can already say for sure that this year's wine has been saved. Alexandrine is sure of that."

"Keep the cases, Virgile. You deserve them as much as I."

"Mr. Massepain gave me four, as well."

"He's a gentleman. Let's go in. Elisabeth must be waiting for us to eat. I think she prepared a beef *estouffade* with olives, mushrooms, and a good red wine—a Canon-Fronsac she managed to steal from me."

Before sitting down, Benjamin grabbed a book from the shelf and handed it to his assistant.

"Here, Virgile, it's a pleasure for me to give you this. You may not care to read Montaigne, and you might frown on Montesquieu, but you must read François Mauriac."

"Maltaverne. That's an intriguing title."

"It's a fine text. I'll be honest with you. I would give anything to have never read it, so I could enjoy discovering it again. Indeed, that is the only advantage of youth."

"Thank you. I'll start reading it tonight."

"Read it whenever you want, Virgile. Tonight, in a week, in a year. It doesn't matter. Great writing is like a great wine. It finds those deserving of it."

Thank you for reading Treachery in Bordeaux.

We invite you to share your thoughts and reactions on Goodreads and your favorite social media and retail platforms.

We appreciate your support.

THE WINEMAKER DETECTIVE SERIES

A total Epicurean immersion in French countryside and gourmet attitude with two expert winemakers turned amateur sleuths gumshoeing around wine country. The following titles are currently available in English.

Grand Cru Heist

In another Epicurean journey in France, renowned wine critic Benjamin Cooker's world gets turned upside down one night in Paris. He retreats to the region around Tours to recover. There a flamboyant British dandy, a spectacular blue-eyed blond, a zealous concierge, and touchy local police disturb his well-deserved rest. From the Loire Valley to Bordeaux, in between a glass of Vouvray and a bottle of Saint-Émilion, the Winemaker Detective and his assistant Virgile turn PI to solve two murders and very particular heist. Who stole those bottles of grand cru classé?

www.grandcruheist.com

Nightmare in Burgundy

The Winemaker Detective leaves his native Bordeaux for Burgundy for a dream wine tasting trip to France's other key wine-making region. Between Beaune, Dijon and Nuits-Saint-Georges, it urns into a troubling nightmare when he stumbles upon a mystery revolving around messages from another era. What do they mean? What dark secrets from the deep past are haunting the Clos de Vougeot? Does blood need to be shed to sharpen people's memory?

www.nightmareinburgundy.com

ABOUT THE AUTHORS

Noël Balen (left) and Jean-Pierre Alaux (right).
(©David Nakache)

Jean-Pierre Alaux and Noël Balen came up with the winemaker detective over a glass of wine, of course. Jean-Pierre Alaux is a magazine, radio, and television journalist when he is not writing novels in southwestern France. He is a genuine wine and food lover and won the Antonin Carême prize for his cookbook *La Truffe sur le Soufflé*, which he wrote with chef Alexis Pélissou. He is the grandson of a winemaker and exhibits a real passion for wine and winemaking. For him, there is no greater common denominator than wine. Series coauthor Noël Balen lives in Paris, where he spends his time writing, making records, and lecturing on music. He plays bass, is a music critic, and has authored a number of books about musicians, in addition to his novel and short-story writing.

ABOUT THE TRANSLATOR

Anne Trager
(©Lebenoist)

Anne Trager has lived in France for over twenty-six years, working in translation, publishing, and communications. In 2011, she woke up one morning and said, "I just can't stand it anymore. There are way too many good books being written in France not reaching a broader audience." That's when she founded Le French Book to translate some of those books into English. The company's motto is "If we love it, we translate it," and Anne loves crime fiction.

MORE BOOKS FROM LE FRENCH BOOK

www.lefrenchbook.com

The 7th Woman by Frédérique Molay

An edge-of-your-seat mystery set in Paris, where beautiful sounding names surround ugly crimes that have Chief of Police Nico Sirsky and his team on tenterhooks.

www.the7thwoman.com

The Paris Lawyer by Sylvie Granotier

A psychological thriller set between the sophisticated corridors of Paris and a small backwater in central France, where rolling hills and quiet country life hide dark secrets.

www.theparislawyer.com

The Greenland Breach by Bernard Besson

The Arctic ice caps are breaking up. Europe and the East Coast of the United States brace for a tidal wave. A team of freelance spies face a merciless war for control of discoveries that will change the future of humanity.

www.thegreenlandbreach.com

The Bleiberg Project by David Khara

Are Hitler's atrocities really over? Find out in this adrenaline-pumping ride to save the world from a conspiracy straight out of the darkest hours of history.

www.thebleibergproject.com

CPSIA information can be obtained at www.ICGtesting.com
Printed in the USA
BVOW11s1201160514

353745BV00013B/231/P